THE NIGHTMARE WHISPERERS

The Gifted Ones have the uncanny ability to enter into people's dreams and control them, implanting subconscious ideas, invoking nightmares. As boys, Dominic Lynch and Patrick Robson were kept as virtual prisoners and their skills exploited for military purposes. When Patrick escapes, it's only to another kind of prison. However, his talent is used for corporate espionage, although he has his own agenda. Yet neither man can escape the corruption their power brings.

Books by John Burke
in the Linford Mystery Library:

THE GOLDEN HORNS
THE POISON CUPBOARD
THE DARK GATEWAY
FEAR BY INSTALMENTS
MURDER, MYSTERY AND MAGIC
ONLY THE RUTHLESS CAN PLAY
THE KILL DOG

JOHN BURKE

THE NIGHTMARE WHISPERERS

Complete and Unabridged

LINFORD
Leicester

First published in Great Britain

First Linford Edition
published 2013

A catalogue record for this book is available
from the British Library.

ISBN 978–1–4448–1581–8

Published by
F. A. Thorpe (Publishing)
Anstey, Leicestershire

Set by Words & Graphics Ltd.
Anstey, Leicestershire
Printed and bound in Great Britain by
T. J. International Ltd., Padstow, Cornwall

This book is printed on acid-free paper

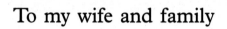

To my wife and family

Be as it will, I have the skill
To work by good or work by ill;
Then here's for pain and here's for thrall,
And here's for conscience, worst of all.
     — James Hogg: *A Witch's Chant*

Part One

DANSE MACABRE

1

The last outgoing flight of the day had long ago taken off on its way to some package-tour holiday island, and residents of Prestwick could settle down for the night. Only some light sleepers might be interrupted by the throbbing roar of a non-scheduled plane coming in low over the sea and then skimming the rooftops. Among those few workers still awake and ready for work in the airport services area were a handful of men within a squat white warehouse whose western wall declared it in large red lettering to be the premises of Steerforth Import/Export Freight. It was an ideal set-up for a secret installation. The double doors, sound-proof walls and lack of windows were commonplace. No flickers of suspicion, because everybody was suspicious as a matter of training, wary of asking questions in case someone turned on them and started nosing into their own set-up.

Brigadier Duncan Muir felt the familiar flutter of anticipation deep down in his guts. Less menacing than the old days of dawn offensives or lightning raids on a Taliban outpost, but full of creepier uncertainties. He wasn't looking forward to seeing what they might be bringing this time; yet the distaste was by now part of the deeper meaning of his job, making it easier for him to authorize the pain for others to inflict.

From the moment the rendition plane touched down one could normally expect delivery of the consignment within ten minutes. He had already double-checked the waiting team, but as a matter of routine he nodded curtly at one after the other, as if to warn them not to doze off. This might be an office job with a mixture of military and civilian personnel, but Muir liked to keep up a parade ground atmosphere, snapping out brief commands to keep them up to scratch, and awake.

With the exception of Dominic Lynch, of course. He would be expected to go to sleep the moment the incoming victim was in place. How he could achieve that to order was a mystery to Muir. Wonderful self-discipline, he supposed — but not the sort of discipline that came into any military training manual.

'All set, Claxton?'

'Of course, sir.'

'The room double-checked, Slee?'

'Very comfortable, sir. Or at any rate,' he leered, 'fit for purpose.'

Lieutenant Petroc Slee often gave the Brigadier the shivers. All right, you needed tough operatives in a tough, dirty campaign; but there was something basically sadistic about the younger man that went beyond the battle savagery of a good fighting man. Slee had been sent home from Afghanistan a year ago pending an investigation into newspaper revelations about repeated torture of a prisoner. The investigation was allowed to drag on until the media grew tired of asking questions and getting only vague replies. The Logistic Corps lieutenant had virtually disappeared from active duty, to undertake a more confidential extension of his duties. His enjoyment in these new activities would seem to confirm that the accusations against him had been justified.

Brigadier Muir carried out his own part without wallowing in it. Invalided out after action in Iraq, he had been assigned to a confidential job in MI6. He had hoped eventually to replace the powerful 'C'; but when the time came he was sidelined into what he had been assured was a challenging job in a new department to be known as the ICB — Information Clearing Bureau. It was not honest face-to-face, hand-to-hand fighting, or even organised shelling and aerial bombardment. Nor did his description as Divisional Coordinator have the flattering mystique of those enviable letters, the C and the M and the Q. But he had been appointed to this post, and therefore he would make it work.

The sound of the buzzer brought Slee and Claxton to their feet. Muir pressed the button in the desk, and they heard the faint hiss of doors opening and closing, and the rumble of wheels along the corridor.

The 'in transit' delivery had arrived.

On the trolley was a large metal box, big enough to hold a man — if he was squeezed in without much room to move.

One of the two CIA men accompanying the consignment passed an envelope to Muir. 'Give him your special overnight treatment before we carry him on to Morocco. That's the form, right?'

'Quite correct.'

The two men were staring at Dominic Lynch, who was in his turn staring at the box, as if to penetrate its secrets before it was even unlocked.

'This is your . . . special operative?' They were not the first to feel dubious about the scrawny young man with his air of epicene remoteness. 'Wouldn't frighten *me*.'

'He's the one who cracked that rendition from Diego Garcia,' said Slee.

'That so?' The man looked more respectful. 'We heard a few details from London station, and — say, didn't he manage to wipe somebody right out as well?'

'One subject did have a heart attack. Unfortunate.'

'Careless. Supposed to be somebody else's assignment.' He shrugged, and turned his attention to the box. 'Right, here's your next course. Hope you've got a very special menu lined up.'

The two men each slid a bolt and swung back a side of the box.

There was a man inside, with arms twisted behind his back and shackled legs doubled up beneath. From under the hood pulled over his head he let out a long, shuddering groan as he was pulled out and thrown to the floor.

'Stand up.'

He rolled over on his side, his arms jerking uselessly. When the hood was wrenched off it revealed a dark, heavily bearded face. One eye was swollen and surrounded by a blue-black pulp, and there was a fine red mark like a ligature biting into his neck.

'This character isn't being very forth-coming. Anything you can find out while he's here, that'll sure be a bonus.'

'A bit of healthy stretching of the limbs?' suggested Slee.

'Stretch 'em too far, and how do we get

him tucked back into the box?'

They all laughed. It eased the strain they had been hardened to avoid feeling too acutely, too often.

'What's been done to him so far?' asked Slee.

'We don't keep a detailed record of each stage of what we call corrective training. Might be misinterpreted if it fell into the wrong hands.'

'So the condition he's in now is due to a few misunderstandings, nothing more?'

'Misunderstandings on his part, yeah.' The taller of the two men had the lazy voice of someone who had rehearsed a bit part for a B-movie. 'Can rile a guy when he gets too stubborn for his own good. Some of the lower ranks can let things run away with 'em.' He winked at Muir. 'You know how it is.'

'No,' said Muir, 'I don't. Not personally.'

'Right on, sir. That's just the way it is. 'Not personally', right? We aim to keep it quite impersonal. Don't want it to go pear-shaped like with those three in Guantánamo Bay. Three guys suffocated.

Official handout was they committed suicide. Couldn't take any more of the interrogation, so hanged themselves. Don't want that to happen on your premises, do we? And what we don't see for ourselves doesn't have to have happened, OK?'

'Least of all when it's happening in his dreams,' added his colleague. 'I mean, who's going to believe *that?*'

He glanced sceptically at Dominic Lynch, who looked blank, as if none of them had anything whatsoever to do with him.

Yet was he, Muir wondered, like blotting paper, soaking in more than the rest of them could guess?

'Hey, look at the inside of this crate.'

'Some of these guys have filthy habits,' said Slee.

'You'd oblige by getting him hosed down. And make sure his face gets a good swilling to freshen him up. And a mouthwash, to leave a nice taste for him. But your main thing right now is to employ these techniques of yours' — scepticism crept back into the tone of voice — 'to ready him for what's waiting. He's been complaining of sleep deprivation. Now you're offering him a whole night's sleep, right? And you make sure he comes out of it shattered before we move him on to the next real questioning. You got the programme?'

Slee said: 'A preview of the usual fingernails and waterboarding, of course. Plus some pretty pictures of a new trick that's waiting for him at the other end.' His fingers clenched and unclenched; a touch of spittle gleamed on his lower lip. 'Every detail supplied by our friends in the Pakistani ISI.'

'Their Inter-Services Intelligence Directorate — yeah, very cooperative guys, aren't they? So you got satisfactory working contact there as well?'

'We have indeed.'

'Right. Let's get our bad boy settled in for the night, shall we?'

They kicked the prisoner repeatedly, dragged him to his feet. Slee and Claxton went with them to show them the bed that had been prepared, with straps to fasten the man down. Then his escorts were shown their own more comfortable quarters. Food and drinks were available in the refrigerator. Music was available at the touch of a switch.

'Pleasant dreams,' said Slee.

'Never you mind about us. Just see that our friend there gets his dream quota. And the hell with it being pleasant.'

Muir summed up for his own team.

'Right, Lynch.' The others always called the young man Dominic as if to ensure that he stayed friendly; but the Brigadier wanted protocol to stay the way it ought to be. 'Everything clear? Ready to start?'

'Ready.'

Muir cleared his throat aggressively. 'The basic idea is to give the man dreams of what's waiting for him when we ship him to our friends in Morocco. Dreams that make everything seem worse than the reality, right?' Anticipation before an attack was nearly always worse than the actual battle. Break the man with visions of the torture before it actually began. It wasn't an idea that Muir really found palatable. Not what he had learned during his military career. But that was how campaigns were fought now. 'Better go and get yourself comfortable.'

'And make our guest well and truly

uncomfortable,' said Slee. An idea suddenly struck him. 'Look, there's no danger of these foretastes immunizing him against all the things you're throwing at him? Defeat the whole purpose.'

'No danger,' said Dominic Lynch with a sagging sneer of the lip.

His voice was as pallid as his complexion. No battle school training, thought Muir with disgust. No P.T., nothing to stiffen him up, put colour in his cheeks and a military tautness in his responses. Muir had raised questions about him early on, and been slapped down. Lynch was too delicate a part of the machinery to be blunted by routine discipline.

'Want me to come with you?' Slee was saying. 'Settle you down comfortably, eh? Swap a couple of bedtime stories about the stories you're going to tell our guest. You've got it all clear about the build-up? Make him feel what it could be like, being flayed alive. And maybe get him dancing on some hot coals at the same time. And singing. Maybe we'll hear him from here and join in the chorus.'

Lynch wasn't looking at him. He rarely

looked directly at anybody. Except, one supposed, when he was at work — at work meaning asleep. Now he glanced at his watch, got up, and sauntered away without a word.

Slee let out a contemptuous laugh as Lynch shut the door behind him. 'I still don't feel he's got the guts. If he does try that flaying idea, or the simple old electric probe routine — '

'No,' snapped Muir. 'You're out of order, Lieutenant. You don't tell *me*. My brief is that this country does *not* condone torture. You know damn well that I must not hear in detail exactly what you're doing. Sooner or later there may be an inquiry. I may have to appear, and I have to be able to say honestly that I have never personally authorized torture. Nor would I condone it, administered by any colleagues or military allies.'

'Sir.' It was insolent rather than respectful. 'Just what do you think is going on along there, along that corridor?'

'I have to administer questioning of a prisoner, but no sort of physical violence. That has always been laid down.' He quoted, trying to believe every word as he uttered it: 'The security services in our country do not practise torture, they do not endorse torture, they don't encourage others to torture on our behalf, they don't collude in torture. That's the way it is, and don't let anybody suggest different.'

'Quite so, sir. And who's going to believe that we're giving that poor bugger a lot of nasty dreams? And once he's been carted off and rendered to someone in Morocco, or Pakistan, or Timbuctoo, what's that got to do with us?' Slee glanced at the tray with its bottle of whisky and glasses, and raised a questioning eyebrow. When Muir did not frown, he took it as permission to pour two large shots. 'You don't have to worry, sir. Your conscience is in the clear. But just what the hell does go on in that trance when Lynch gets cracking? Creepy, isn't it?'

Muir clutched his glass and took a long sip. 'Look,' he said, 'do you really think these wretched creatures who get channelled through here have anything really to tell us? Or,' he added hastily, 'to tell the folk at the other end?'

'We have to find out. That's what the job's about, isn't it?'

'But if any of them come out with any old crap, just to stop the torture — '

'Hold it, sir. We've agreed that we are not complicit in torture.'

'Whatever you call it. Nothing that creature along there says is necessarily going to be true. For all we know, Lynch might be — '

'Planting ideas of his own in the sucker's mind? That thought's already occurred to me. But we must just carry out the routine as instructed, right? Fill in the usual forms and keep our noses clean.'

Muir was grateful for the warming Scotch, which was beginning to soothe away uneasy speculations; but at the same time he was unhappy with the company, wondering again whether Slee was a plant, put here to trip him up and report back to their unfathomable Section Chief in London.

Another uneasy question went unspoken. It was no more than a sneaky feeling that it might be wise for the rest of them to stay awake while Dominic was operating. They didn't want him to stumble into their own dreams, to inflict on them what in the field was known as 'friendly fire'.

★ ★ ★

Afterwards, in the dawn, the plane took off. Its passenger list, a short and secret one, included a gibbering wreck of a man heading for a three-dimensional demonstration of what had menaced him during the night.

The others yawned and waited for Muir to order the stand-down.

Dominic Lynch looked utterly drained, yet satisfied.

'You feel OK?' Slee's tone of voice suggested he wanted to disturb that complacency.

Dominic nodded.

'Just how did you get to the bastard?' Slee persisted. 'What exactly did you . . . well, *think* into him? That's the way you operate, isn't it?'

Dominic yawned. 'It was fairly straightforward.'

'But — '

'Enough,' snapped Muir. 'The job's been done. That's it.'

Slee and Claxton were left to check on the refrigerator, plates and cutlery, strip the beds, take bedclothes to the laundry, and set everything clean and in position for any sudden new rendition arrival. Muir drove Dominic Lynch back to his safe house on the outskirts of Ayr.

Dominic stayed silent. Muir found himself wondering again how, when the whole thrust of the young man's job was to disorientate a prisoner, could he not become infected himself?

Muir knew of more than one case of a seasoned interrogative officer cracking and being hastily sent off for counselling and compassionate retirement. But how could there be any compassion in a world of such deliberate viciousness? When somebody wasn't up to the job and collapsed, you chucked them out and replaced them.

After a light breakfast, Dominic went for another sleep — this time without any commitments.

Muir braced himself for the obligatory

18

summing-up with Sedlák. Somebody else who just didn't belong in his own ordered world, but had been foisted on him. And he was supposed to treat the man with respect — and yet, of course, be cautious. This was a game some officers and undercover men enjoyed. Muir was still uneasy in the company of men whose loyalties even their top-level handlers seemed wary of.

Professor Pavel Sedlák's father had been one of the Czechs who fled to Britain in World War II to join the struggle against the Nazis who had occupied his country. He had been a camouflage expert, and apparently a highly qualified one. When he returned to his homeland after the war, there were conflicting stories about his conduct. Did he work with the Communists or quietly against them? Whichever way he handled it, somehow he managed to survive, and his son Pavel found an apparently safe, innocuous post in the administration; though there were murmurs about an attachment to the STB, the secret police, and to his having been trained in some of the darker secrets of certain rooms, spoken of only in hushed voices, in the notorious Pancraz prison in Prague.

Muir thought it possible that the man could have been a double agent, playing devious games for both sides. After the Velvet Revolution in Czechoslovakia he was brought out to London, conceivably for his own safety. Why he had been assigned to monitoring Dominic Lynch was another of those questions that did not get asked or answered at Muir's level. Were they being infiltrated? There had been cases of a trusted double agent walking into a meeting and blowing the whole lot of them sky-high because they had been too naïve to suspect a treble agent.

This morning the man had received their charge back into their shared house with a squeeze of the arm, settled him down in his room, and then returned to Muir hungry for a briefing.

'It went well, yes? I have taken his pulse, and I think he found it not too much of a strain. Our American friends were not unhappy?'

'The prisoner was damned unhappy. The Yanks were quite impressed.'

'The boy has talent. Remarkable talent. But I worry perhaps it takes too much out of him. We must be sure not to . . . overstretch him.'

Muir tried to restrain his impatience at any hint of mollycoddling during military operations. 'Unlike some of our operatives, he doesn't actually have to get his hands dirty. It's all . . . well, just brainwork.'

'*Just* brainwork? But more fruitful than some of our distant colleagues' attempts, no?

'They do seem impressed.'

'But so I would hope. Their experiments — so amusing, don't you think? Agents staring at goats, attempting long-distance telepathy, believing that perhaps it is physically possible for a man to learn to walk through a brick wall. We are made up of atoms, and walls are made up of atoms, so all you have to do is adjust the spaces so that *your* atoms can slide through. Our American friends,' he grinned, 'must have suffered a lot of bruised faces. Such blundering boys, yes? Still not out of — this is how you say it,

21

yes? — the short pants.'

Muir often did feel just that way about his country's supposed allies.

'But of course,' Sedlák went contentedly on, 'we do have to explore much more sophisticated means of inquiry these days, is it not so? My late father helped to create fortifications which did not exist but which the Germans photographed and believed to be there. And there was clumsy, crude propaganda on the radio and in newspapers.'

'Black propaganda.' Muir was not entirely ignorant of World War II history.

'Whereas today we avoid any crude assault on the mind. Gradually we must build up a mental force as powerful as any army brigade or air force. We develop the powers of this young Mr. Lynch and his kind to convey misinformation directly into the unresisting sleeping minds of the enemy.

'We plant thoughts to confuse them. Plant lies which they have no conscious ability to analyse.'

'Make zombies of them,' said Muir.

'Ah, no. Zombies consume human

flesh, starting from the outside. So does napalm. What we are after is a thought process consuming from *inside*.'

Muir suppressed a yawn. There was really nothing to talk about until Lynch had rested and would be wide-awake for the debriefing. Always assuming he was prepared to answer questions. He could be very awkward, hugging things to his chest.

Sedlák was rambling on. 'But you know, of course, that young Lynch is not alone. There are others with the faculty — the gifted ones. Apparently your people let slip a practitioner superior to this young man.'

'Not my people, damnit. Before I took charge. Some deserter who managed to get one of his pursuers to blow his insides out for starters.' He grimaced. 'That's the sort of killer we could do with on our strength.'

'Strength. Yes, such an important concept. Does this young Dominic have enough? To create fear, does he risk using his own fears — fear of cutting himself while shaving, losing control of a weapon which turns itself against him, losing control . . . '

'Quite an imagination you have there,' Muir grunted.

A door upstairs closed. A stair tread creaked as somebody came down. Sedlák brightened and turned to face the newcomer.

A girl in a pale green dress came in and smiled affectionately at him, and then demurely at Muir. She was about seventeen or eighteen, peach-skinned and glowing with that sort of quiet eagerness which reminded Muir of his own daughter before she took to drugs, rock bands and raucous demos.

'Brigadier Muir,' Sedlák was suddenly formal and correct, 'I think you have not met my daughter Milada, no?'

'No.' Muir stuck out his hand, and was met by the touch of warm, smooth fingers. 'How d'ye do, Miss Sedlák.'

'In our country, the lady is called Sedláková,' said her father.

Well, thought Muir, bristling, she's not in that bloody country now, is she? And what exactly is she doing here, if anything?

2

The river Morava on its long way from the northern slopes of the border hills weaves its way through forests and valleys down to the plain until, approaching the Austrian border, it loops around the village of Cjekovice and into the dreams of Milada Sedláková. Its slow pace here is soothing, so that even when she is awake much of the world around her has the quality of a dream, save that her night world is usually more real.

Not so long ago every wedding or holiday here was celebrated with folk music and dance, strictly monitored by the Communist authorities in the name of uncorrupted Slav tradition. Today young Milada and her friends have a choice. With freedom has come Western pop with its strobe-dazzled raves in village halls and taverns. The local folk group has lost ground to the heavily amplified guitars and electronic keyboards, reverberating down the lanes behind the reopened church and through the bar of the local hospoda. Ten years from now perhaps the polkas and the gypsy songs will be quite forgotten, but for just a while there is a choice. The local school-master still enjoys keeping the old traditions alive for their own sake, and to some extent is helped by the new régime, happy to maintain enough colourful Slav sounds and costumes to boost the growing tourist trade. He had followed official precepts about traditional national trends when they were forced upon the community, and had grown to believe in them. But now?

'We still want the hoary old songs and dances,' he jokes. 'Only now we can enjoy them for their own sakes, not because we are ordered to.'

For Milada her favourite dance is still the weekend one in a wine cellar sunk into the side of a small hill, its entrance painted with a floral design in danger of flaking away. Inside there is still the sound of fiddle, pipes, accordion and cimbalom. And here through her head there still ring the lilting strains of the gypsy song *Kapura, Kapura* and the rhythms of the traditional Girls' Dance.

Her family home in the well-preserved wing of an old château had been allocated to her father in acknowledgment of his work for the State. She knows that locals mutter about exactly what those services of his might have been. In those days of dogma and restrictions he had often been away from home, in Brno or even in Prague. And her mother was rarely mentioned. 'Sad,' was a word she heard from her father's lips and from the lips of villagers, though with different intonations.

Nowadays there are murmurs of him leaving, too. Of taking Milada with him. Being subtly driven out? Still nobody seems keen on voicing the first outright accusation. Professor Pavel Sedlák is now suspected of easing himself into the protection of other manipulators, variously guessed at but not spoken about too brashly.

And his daughter has sometimes been shunned by her school friends and then the girls in the winery where she works in the accounts office. Milada has bright chestnut hair, unusual among the dark-haired Moravian girls long intermingled with Slovak gypsy strains. Some of the local boys are less discriminatory than their sisters, thinking of her only as a beautiful girl, ripe for the plucking. Yet even for them there are hesitations of a different kind, their appetites weakened by wariness. Something about the girl sets her apart. Her contemporaries in the winery call her a dreamer: but not of the kind of dreams they take for granted. They sense that she goes into places they cannot hope to explore, and perhaps wouldn't dare to.

Milada herself is aware of never quite belonging, yet not knowing where she ought to be. 'Giving herself airs,' they mutter. But to her the airs are those of the woods and meadows, the breeze in the pussy willows, the susurration of birds rising in a pirouetting cloud, and always the music that pulses through all creation.

On spring days she wanders through the unkempt grounds of the château, singing gently to herself. She will kneel in a trance under an old maple tree, or sit for hours beside the baroque fountain of a man tipping what looks like a wine cask so that its contents overflow the shallow basin at his feet into a deeper basin below. The water supply has been maintained throughout successive political upheavals, and reassures her with its unquenchable music — a tinkling, plopping, whispering dance rhythm.

Sometimes her wanderings are brought to a halt by the sound of even remoter strains — the ethereal notes of Bartók's 'night music', simple pieces of which she has picked out on the old piano left neglected in the uninhabited end of the château. The echoes stay with her wherever she goes, playing around her, drawing her closer.

Closest of all when she sits beside the stump of an oak tree beside the river, eaten away from one side until she finds she can push her hand through. There ought to be somebody at the other end, waiting to take her hand in his. She closes her eyes, and drowses. The landscape shimmers through her eyelids, and in her ears are the lyrics of the nostalgic

Lavecka with its lament for 'the broken bench where I used to sit with my lover' and its plea, 'Give me back my lover of yesteryear.'

The broken bench reshapes itself into the wooden stump and then into a humped stone. A different waterway drifts past her, a stream rather than a river.

It is from here, half asleep then asleep while still sitting upright, that she realizes for the first time what does truly set her apart from those others. Memories of the previous weekend's dance come back, with the feel of young Lad'a's arm tightening around her, and his clumsily groping hands. There had been laughter and some meaningful remarks when he appeared that evening. Wasn't he usually one of the rowdier lot at the modern discos? But lured here by designs on Milada? No chance, no chance . . .

There had been an hour or so when she had felt warm and responsive, but then she had flinched away; and now is unsure whether she had really wanted to hold back. Confused in a dream of the crowded hall, she suddenly knows that

30

Lad'a himself is back there too — perhaps slumped over his daytime work in the estate office, lost briefly in an afternoon daydream. She feels through her body what his own desires are.

Then he wakes up, jolted back to work. And she is awake again, reaching out for reassurance to the oak stump. Somewhere on the fringe of another dream, still beyond her grasp, there is a man whose touch she must wait for. On her way home she passes Lad'a.

He stares, stumbles, and mutters only the most everyday passing greeting. But that stare tells her that he *knows*. He knows that she was there in his bleary daydream, conscious of exactly what he was feeling. Lad'a is scared. His face goes scarlet, and he blunders away.

Milada finds a new pastime. At night she goes what she calls 'visiting'. It is simpler than she could have imagined: she relaxes into sleep, starts strolling without leaving her bed, and saunters at random into the night worlds of girls she knows, and others she has never met. And stumbles into one she would have avoided if she'd had any warning.

'You bitch! What are you doing here?'

It is Katarina Parkánová, one of the winery girls who is always bringing some new imported disc into the winery and playing the latest fad — grunge, rap or whatever its alien name might be — at full blast. At weekends she was the liveliest in the disco. Lad'a was the local lad she had set her eyes on; and Lad'a was here with her in this dream — dancing to her tune here, if nowhere else.

As Milada fights to free herself from those writhing coils of another's desire and envy, the image of Lad'a fades, escaping both of them.

'Where the hell d'you think you're taking him? Let go. Get your hands off him. Off us. Bitch.'

At work the next day the blowsy young woman's dream face has become even more contorted, venomous.

At last Milada forces herself to conjure up, night after night, a picture of her riverside stump, and concentrate on it with the certainty that she must make it turn into a distant stone. Time after time she floats across the water, over the grass, and glimpses the shape of the man she knows has to be there waiting for her. And time after time the scene will not hold. Sketchy woods and slopes dissolve out of reach. The man is lost in the haze.

Until, one night, her intense concentration works on the wooden stump here and the stone there, and they begin slowly and steadily to overlap — the wood dissolving into a new shape, hardening, growing clearer against a clear new background.

The river Morava has shrunk into a meandering stream, with an elbow twist just like the one around the château.

And at last he is there.

He says: 'Milada.' He has her fingers in his grasp. 'Swear that for one year from this day you will be faithful to me.'

'Only a year?'

'Swear it.'

'I swear. And after that. Forever.' She is looking deep into his eyes, loving the passion within them yet worried by a dark whirlpool in those depths. 'And you . . . ?'

'I will be faithful to you. Handfasted until the year is up. And then we decide whether to continue or whether to part. Without reproach.'

Handfasted. For her it is no question of a year, but for an eternity. In his heart he must surely know already that she is his forever, and their promise cannot be broken or contaminated.

As she drifts reluctantly away, she tries to keep him in focus, but a shadow comes between them, watching both of them, evaluating every word and movement. A guardian — or an enemy?

Night after night she lets her fantasies take hold. She tries to revisit him, but then is ashamed of being so forward. She must be patient: their time will come. Still she wanders, restless, eager to test the extent of her newly revealed powers; and suddenly finds herself sucked into the whirlpool of somebody else's nightmare. It is all incredibly sharp-edged, the clear-cut black and white of the old films, which they still show in the shabby old village cinema. A horror movie this time.

A woman is fettered in a cell, under

irregular drops of water, which must eventually drive her mad. And just as irregular, but louder than the drip of the water, come the questions. Demanding repentance. Demanding the names of fellow conspirators.

'There was nobody. I have done no wrong.'

Milada knows where she is now. This is the hideous heart of Spilberk Castle on the heights of Brno, where centuries of persecution have swallowed up the guilty and innocent indiscriminately. Beside the torture chambers it boasts a sequence of tiny cells in which, whether they had confessed to anything or not, women were finally bricked up and left to rot.

Milada's father has never taken her as far as Brno, but she is now deep in it, knowing it because of what he is showing her. This is her father's dream — his guilty nightmare of the place where evil never dies. The terror of the victims is left on the air, to be picked up by minds attuned to its resonances and re-used, amplified. Misery undying. Like the tortured themselves — racked, wrenched, fouled, close to death but not allowed to die.

In the morning she says: 'You were there, weren't you?'

'My dear, what are you talking about?'

'In that place. That was my mother, wasn't it? And you knew, and you let them do it. You were *there*.'

'No.' He is staring at her the way Lad'a had stared, frightened but trying to keep his voice steady. 'It was an illusion. I did what I could to help her, but she wouldn't listen, and . . . and . . . '

'You let them take Mama. And watched while they — '

'No.' He is sweating. 'That didn't happen. Please, you must not think that was real. What you saw was my nightmare. I did not wish to believe that was the way it was. I tried to protect her, but she had made some serious mistakes, and it was ruled that she should be sent to a Correction Facility. I tried to intervene. But one has to accept the judgment of those who have so many matters to administer.'

'You knew exactly what they would be doing to Mama. They let you visit — and watch?'

'No. What you saw was my imagination. Too much from . . . from things we heard about what the Germans did when they were here. I have had to go along with certain undesirable elements in order to protect *you*, my darling, from a similar fate.'

'They used to burn witches,' says Milada dully. 'Are they still at it?'

'Your mother was no witch. But let's say she was . . . *gifted*.' He is eager to shrug off the horror and clutch at something more rewarding. 'And now we discover that you are in the bloodline. One of the Gifted Ones.' She can almost see the capital letters in his awestruck words. 'One of *them*.' Now he is talking faster and faster, to blot out the torment and make her smile, make her believe in him. 'I think perhaps it is time we look for help elsewhere. There is nothing here for you. I have contacts. People who owe me for what I have contributed. We must leave this place and find others who will make things very comfortable for you.'

She shrinks away from her father's glutinous kiss, but she knows it is indeed time for them to go. To get closer. Not to whoever her father has in mind, but to someone who is waiting.

In her dream she waits for a sign of approval or warning from the tall shadow in the corner of the pasture; but it is impassive, leaving her to make her own decisions, her own mistakes.

Sooner or later you will have to choose.

★   ★   ★

Without warning, without a sound, Dominic was suddenly back in the room. He did not bother to speak to anyone, but settled himself in a chair in the window and stared at Milada.

'Not had much of a nap, lad,' Muir accused him.

Dominic shrugged and did not take his eyes off the girl. Muir wondered sourly whether he might perhaps be tickling his way into *her* dreams.

Sedlák leaned forward to break the spell between his daughter and the young man. 'We have just been talking about an old school friend of yours. That very

38

special school. There was one like yourself . . . ' He waited as if counting two or three beats, then said lightly: 'Perhaps one even more . . . specialized.'

Dominic Lynch answered with apparent indifference. 'Patrick Robson. That the one? Wouldn't say he was all that much ahead.'

'But you do sometimes . . . shall we say, *communicate* with him?'

Muir had no intention of letting Sedlák take charge. 'Look, lad, if you know where he is, it's your duty to get in touch and bring him over to us.'

'No, I don't know where he is. He has put up his own firewall. There is no way in.'

'Can't you bloody well *find* a way in?'

'Perhaps it might be possible to come across him roaming one night.' Dominic's eye drooped lazily. 'I haven't bothered so far.'

Muir was convinced he was lying. 'Then *start* bothering. We need all the troops we can muster. Get on your broomstick and find him, understood?'

It was difficult to tell whether Milada

Sedláková was listening or not, and understanding or not. She appeared quite contented, sitting there with a remote smile as if not wanting to join in but simply allowing words — perhaps largely in a foreign language to her — to roll over her.

'*Find* him,' Muir repeated. 'Get a hold on him *somehow*.'

Milada's smile deepened, daydreaming of something or someone far away. Or perhaps far away no longer.

3

The head offices of Copsholm Communications had for the past five years been installed in a building more in tune with historic conflicts than with modern commercial campaigns. Burntbrigg Hall had once been a bleak 16th-century pele tower fortified against reiving raids from across the Scottish Border. Twice burnt out by attackers and rebuilt with even heavier walls and a turret giving wider views over the moors, it was neglected in more peaceful times until a Northumbrian squire favoured at Court was granted land around it, and set about making himself and his family comfortable. He retained the tower as the endpiece of a Jacobean grange, and added more generous windows to the turret. A large walled garden and an ornamental gateway to the south were approached between showy box hedges designed mainly to impress the visitor.

Ruth Saltram never failed to enjoy the gently climbing road as she drove in each morning. The day's work could provide a dozen frustrations, and by evening she might be anxious to get out of the place and drive doggedly back across the Shire to her cottage in a secluded corner of the town; but on a sunny morning the sight of that coffee-brown stone and red-brick building poised so elegantly above the stream was always fresh and welcoming.

Today they all needed to be wide-awake when the client arrived. This had to be a skilful sales pitch, convincing him without giving away too much about their most powerful asset.

She parked in her usual slot, observing that Bethany's white Hyundai and Matthew's red Jag were already there ahead of her. Another two, tense and persuading themselves that an early arrival would somehow make things easier. Somebody — probably Hugo, always on the premises and always up early — had fixed a large notice above a slot in the visitors' car park: RESERVED FOR MR ROGER SNAPE. Not that anybody else was expected today.

Ruth checked in the driving mirror that her lipstick and hair had not been disturbed during the drive. Her hair had gone a speckled grey early, yet gave her an incongruously young, trim look. She felt reasonably confident of being fit to face the day.

As she crossed the gravel square towards the entrance, she glanced up at the turret. Morning sunlight slashed a dazzling arc across the mullioned widow, but she glimpsed a face peering out for a moment, then vanishing. It looked as if Patrick was up early for once, though there was no likelihood of his being summoned to the meeting. He was not for public exhibition. His part would come later.

She went to her office and indulged in her pre-conference routine. A ritual five minutes of stillness, sitting upright at her desk and breathing rhythmically. Then she would tidy the array of pens and notepads along the far edge of the desk, even though this had already been done for her by Bethany the previous afternoon before leaving, and finally reach into the small refrigerator set into the desk close to her right knee and pour herself a glass of cold water.

Now she could relax in her familiar surroundings and permit the working day to begin.

Ruth Saltram had begun her professional life as secretary to the advertising manager of a magazine group. Her then sleek brown hair and the sloe-dark depths of her eyes caught the attention of one of their regular photographers, who suggested using her in a fashion piece. She had no ambition to become a model, having already met too many of them during her career, but was not too displeased by the reactions of contemporaries to her appearance on the cover of one of the company's magazines.

'Using their own staff to save paying full rate for a professional.' sneered one rival publication.

Against which you could set the fulsome approaches of two editors and one PR recruitment agency, plus flattering amorous attempts by three colleagues.

Within the next month she was forced

to make a choice between promotion within her own group and the headhunting PR agency in Newcastle-upon-Tyne. She had been happily to school in Tynemouth, and in a moment of nostalgia chose the Newcastle agency. Six months later she married its managing director. They made a smart, much envied and much sought-after couple for promotion parties, first nights, and literary award functions throughout the region. The only snag was that her husband's first wife still possessed a major shareholding in the company, and spent her spare time making difficulties at board meetings and leaking information to rivals. When the time came for a takeover by a company trading as Copsholm Consultants, the resultant clash left Ruth battling against her husband and her relentless predecessor. She won, eased them out, left them both behind to resume their own quarrelsome relationship, and in the resulting amalgamation instigated the name change of the company to Copsholm Communications: she had always found something intrinsically seedy about the very word and whole concept of 'consultancy'. She then recommended moving head office to the impressive setting of Burntbrigg Hall.

Financial commentators predicted disaster. How could a modern company, needing to be close to everything that was going on in the business and promotional world, expect clients to travel out into the Northumbrian countryside for discussions; and how could its executives hope to keep in touch with events the moment they happened — or, preferably, before they happened?

'We have every modern facility for keeping in touch,' Matthew Armour announced in a press release. 'And my colleague Ruth Saltram is introducing specialized facilities of her own to outguess anybody else in the field.'

There had been some talk in the trade that their partnership wouldn't last long. 'Company's not big enough for two tough operators on that level.' But Ruth quietly manoeuvred Matthew into a situation where he would either have to give damaging battle for the leadership, resign, or tacitly agree to play second fiddle.

Matthew Armour stayed on, with the two of them presenting an amicable relationship to their competitors and potential clients.

'Good morning, Ruth.'

As usual, Matthew had rapped hard on her door before walking in without an invitation. It was one of his remaining ways of asserting himself. Others tapped quietly and waited to be summoned in.

'Good morning, Matt.' She didn't look up until he had settled into a chair opposite. 'Happy with the programme?'

'I've been going over it again. Spent some time last night . . . '

When she did glance across at him, she could see the familiar redness in his eyes, an after-effect of stooping over his laptop. Matthew had built up his original firm by gruelling hard work, accumulating facts, afraid of missing some crucial little point, sweating himself into a fever of concentration. In his hands there were few clumsy errors or oversights; but he was incapable of great flights of the imagination — indeed, distrusted any such fantasies.

Behind him, Bethany Critchley slid into the room, sleek in a floral tunic and black skirt. She had done her jet-black hair as carefully as Ruth's, smoothly assuming her role for the day. She always presented a languid confidence, good at distracting male clients by her faintly condescending smile and by careful adjustment of her long legs. She could never be mistaken for a mere secretary, merely taking notes. In any case, the recorder built into the table preserved all their discussions. Bethany maintained the air of a fellow consultant, watchful and always permitted to contribute.

'Right, then.' Matthew put on his masterful air of calling a huge meeting to order. 'We've got to play this clever. We very nearly lost that French deal last September because of overplaying the delicacy line of their male toning lotion rather than its masculinity.'

'Wouldn't have been much of a loss anyway,' observed Bethany. 'Not one of their more prestigious products.'

'Didn't stop you collaring samples for your boyfriend, did it, Betty?' Matthew smirked.

Bethany hated being called Betty. He fancied it was a good-humoured way of keeping her in her place.

'Anyway,' said Ruth firmly, 'let's concentrate on persuading our friend from Valence that he's dealing with a job already polished to perfection in our own minds.'

'A snooty bit of work,' Matthew recalled. 'The best way to handle him is to let him think he's caught us out in a minor detail, and then there's bags of digs in the ribs, and we all pretend he's spotted something vital and set us really and truly on the right lines.'

Bethany, standing by the window, said: 'His car's just rolling up. And it *is* a Roller.'

They moved across the corridor to the conference room.

★   ★   ★

Roger Snape was a stocky man running to fat who relieved the sober charcoal grey of his suit and pale blue shirt with a discreetly striped tie of the kind that vaguely suggested membership of a club. He liked to saunter into a room and look all around in one leisurely glance that made it clear he was capable of summing up a whole situation within seconds and was not a man prepared to be bored by any irrelevancies.

He was accompanied by a willowy blonde in an aqua-blue cape fastened at the neck with a large buckle. She and Bethany eyed one another with courteous mistrust, measuring the possible rivalry.

There was a flurried interchange of names of which only the blonde's was new to the scene.

'Zoë.' Snape raised his right hand briskly, combining easygoing comradeship with the emphasis of one who must be seen to be in command.

She obediently opened her large, flat briefcase, drew out a number of coloured sketches of bottles and tubes, and set them reverently in front of him.

'I think we're agreed, after that last campaign that old-fashioned methods are no use today. There were one or two aspects that seemed just a little bit feeble in the light of more aggressive approaches shown by our rivals.'

'I understood,' said Matthew, immediately defensive, 'that your sales increased by seventy-five per cent. Didn't I read that in your annual report?'

'That's true. But there was a certain element of left-over momentum from the previous year's trading, plus the goodwill our name always carries. But don't think I'm nitpicking.' Snape beamed benevolently at the three facing him. 'All I want to emphasize is that it's the view of my fellow directors that we should do something more up-to-date, more subtle. Sort of *creep up* on the customer without too blatant a message.' His gaze settled on Ruth. 'You did give the impression when we spoke on the phone that you have been experimenting with some highly specialized new facilities. Quite unique. But' — he tipped his head knowingly to one side — 'we've heard hints from elsewhere that you might be letting other chosen clients have the benefit of it.'

So a whisper had got round the trade, thought Ruth. Some hint of something very special that Copsholm had applied for another customer's benefit? She was none too upset. She said: 'We like to think so. Direct advertising to the general public is too crude nowadays. Big blatant promotions are defeating their own object — colour ads in the glossies, on poster sites, on television. The public is growing suspicious, too, of articles by fashion correspondents whose supposedly unbiased views have too obviously been paid for.'

'Free meals and expensive handbags,' added Matthew.

'So your plans for our new product?' Snape pointed a drooping finger at the spread of colour pictures on the table, and the well-trained Zoë reshuffled them into a fresh order, giving prominence to a photograph of a large pot of skin cream. At the same time Snape produced an actual pot and placed it reverently in the centre of the display, smiling at Bethany Critchley and indicating that she should open it. 'A quite wonderful development. A blend of spicy notes — saffron and ginger, sandalwood . . . and a secret ingredient which adds a piquancy that . . . ' He raised a questioning eyebrow, waiting for Bethany's judgment.

She said: 'It's gorgeous. Really gorgeous. But so . . . well . . . '

'Subtle, wouldn't you say?'

'It does . . . well, yes, keep you waiting, if that's the way to put it.'

'Admirably put, young lady. And let me be quite honest. We have quite deliberately developed a blend that has a mildly hypnotic effect. Once bought, the reorders will keep coming.'

'I'd be a bit worried about any element of illegal drugs.' Matthew decided it was time to sound decisive.

'We've been careful. There's no element of dangerous addiction. Just a lure as compelling as one's favourite flowers, or choice Italian dish . . . '

Over Snape's shoulder Ruth caught glimpses of the world beyond the window. A succession of scudding clouds were playing games with the sun, filtering its light and then letting it spray forth in sudden bursts. The view was in danger of becoming hypnotic, like the face cream that the man Snape was going on about.

'Mrs. Saltram . . . ?'

The pot was slid along the table. Ruth

dipped a finger in. The scent that came up was penetrating yet gentle. She had to nod an agreement.

'Subtle?' Snape trotted the word out again. 'A lot more to commend it than some Knightsbridge concoction at nine hundred quid a throw, hm?'

'And I do get your point,' Matthew hurried to say. 'Our advertising campaign has to be just as subtle. Something as intriguing as the product itself. Insinuating. Subtle, yes.'

'But none of that subliminal stuff,' Snape warned. 'Shoving millisecond mumbles into telly programmes and hoping to hypnotize the viewers. We had enough trouble with that on an earlier campaign.'

'Not with us,' rasped Matthew.

'No. Before we joined forces.' Snape smiled magnanimously.

Ruth said: 'Right. Let's agree that the current agreement to allow blatant product placement in everyday TV programmes is not for us. But have we come to the end of implanting messages in mobiles? Google has been selling targeted advertising via an auction system. And there's been some market research establishing mobile and iPod owners' particular interests. One could insinuate our message into a thousand Facebook projections. Imply that some important person is using our product.'

A CCTV camera in the far corner, masquerading as a wall light, was recording the client's facial expressions, on which Ruth set great store. She also found it useful for interpreting some of Matthew's grimaces, seeing where his mind was going. At the moment it was presumably recording his calculatedly confident expression.

'Whatever the spiel' — Snape used the word with a self-conscious shrug, 'some of my publicity team have ideas about the way wording can be balanced to impress readers and viewers without them quite realizing it. Especially in the weekend fashion magazines. Carefully calculated to stand out from the outdated clichés all around it. Such as page after page of cleavage. Though more recently it's navels, isn't it?' He glanced archly at Bethany's midriff as if hoping to see through the fabric of her dress.

His words fell into an awkward silence.

'Time for coffee?' Matthew was at any rate alert to the appropriate timing. 'And perhaps a small mid-morning sherry?'

'A very small sherry wouldn't come amiss,' said Snape. 'I wouldn't want poor Zoë to have to drive us back,' he added archly.

When the cups and glasses had been distributed, Ruth decided to keep the conversation general before they edged closer to Copsholm's specific plans.

'I think we can be frank about one aspect of our work. Marketing by what one may call hidden persuasion has become the dominant force in human culture today. Almost nothing people think and feel gets there by mere chance. After all, human beings have only a certain number of appetites, and what we have to do is relate these psychologically as closely as possible to products it's in our interest to make them buy.'

'Without triggering their resistance to marketing influences,' said Snape knowingly. 'And' — he sipped his sherry and put the glass down with a smug nod — 'getting at the largest possible number without coarsening the approach. Exactly what plans do you have, Mrs Saltram, for doing that?'

'Flooding the whole public mind is not practicable. It's no good shouting our wares at the tops of our voices in an old-fashioned marketplace — or, today, on one telly ad after another, all ablaze with colour and loud music and voices chanting orders at you. On the other hand, one can't *whisper* suggestions to every potential customer in the country. One must infiltrate gradually. Reach into the minds of the men and women at the top: the managing directors, the managers, the buyers, the fashion gurus. Let *them* spread the gospel with compelling sincerity because they genuinely believe what we've programmed them to believe.'

'And just what gimmick do you have for doing that?'

'Not a gimmick,' said Ruth.

'One of our little trade secrets,' said Matthew. 'Commercial confidentiality, you know.'

'Yes, but look, this is quite a special deal. Valence is doing the paying — '

'You pay us for the result. We keep the know-how.'

Snape was still looking at Ruth. She said: 'We got results in that last campaign, didn't we?'

'I have to admit I still don't quite see how you did that. That managing director . . . how the devil did you swing him? We'd had some of our best reps working on that man over the years, but he'd always been too persuasion-proof.'

'You could say it was by telepathy. Like I said, planting an idea directly into the minds of the most influential people. Though our own technique is more rarefied than that.'

Matthew fidgeted, fearful of her giving away their secret, yet wanting to let it be seen just how thoroughly he was in the know.

'Well, then.' Snape saw he would be getting no special revelations. He gave Zoë another of his jerky nods, which she was obviously skilled at interpreting. A sheaf of documents appeared. 'We've got a very nasty rival on our heels,' he revealed, 'fancying the chances of a takeover. We

58

need to show him we don't need him.' For a moment he looked as worried as Matthew had been about a possibly unwise revelation, and rushed on: 'Right, then. Right. Let's be quite sure about the basic parameters and the costing . . .'

When they had ploughed through the run-of-the-mill facts and figures, and Snape and his assistant had driven off, Ruth said: 'This is definitely up Patrick's street. We've got to work out a campaign within his capabilities.' She got up from the table as Bethany began gathering up the prints Snape had brought.

'Off to discuss it with his keeper?' said Matthew sourly. 'Get the lad in the mood. He can take a lot of pampering, that one.'

She was beginning to wonder if the time was near when she would have to find a way of easing Matthew out of their partnership — or, if he wasn't willing to be eased out, then thrown out.

4

Patrick's eyrie was reached up a wheel stair in the turret, its medieval constriction made tighter by the tricky installation of a stairlift track. At the bottom was a modern door, usually kept locked. Not that Patrick seemed likely to want to escape. He seemed perfectly content up there, alone with books, television, and the music, which he would listen to for hours on end.

Ruth found the door at the foot of the stairs open, and edged past the bulky rail of the stairlift towards the half-landing. On the third step she felt a sudden stab of cold air, as if a draught from outside had cut through a hole in the stonework. But there was no gap there, and the weather outside was sunny and warm. If she turned her head, would she see some faint, misty figure . . . a ghost? Of course Burntrigg Hall ought to have its traditional ghost. Ruth Saltram didn't believe in such things; but was irritated by the suspicion that this unease might be a malicious telepathic joke of Patrick's, in spite of Hugo having assured her that Patrick's gift was something quite distinct from mere telepathy.

Faintly from above she heard a wispy thread of music, which she knew enough of his austere tastes by now to guess that it must be something by Berg or Webern.

As she stepped from the first arc of the stair into the first-floor flat, Hugo rose from his desk to meet her, coolly affable as usual.

Dr. Hugo Lanner had a lean, ascetic face with a faintly olive complexion and melancholy eyes. His rare smile had the stoicism of a man who has seen too much but is complacent about his own fortitude. He dressed untidily, yet managed to look expensive and beyond criticism. His main vanity was the shine on his brown brogues, which must obviously have been given a scrupulous polishing each morning. In meetings he had a habit of stretching out his legs and contemplating the shoes as if hoping to catch his own reflection in their impeccable gloss.

His nod to his secretary, who had been

taking notes from him into a laptop, signified that she should leave.

Carolyn Finch-Mordaunt always combined politeness with a slight hint of superiority in her smile at Ruth. She had adopted some of Bethany Critchley's mannerisms to convey the idea of being something loftier than a secretary — Dr. Lanner's research assistant, as it were.

Lanner waited for Ruth to settle in the window-seat.

'Right, tell me the worst. How much pressure will we have to put him under this time?'

She explained the basic facts behind the Valence approach. She and Matthew were hopeful that this one shouldn't be too difficult for Patrick.

'Might there be some way of getting into the minds of . . . well, some senior figure in the trade? Head buyer for one of the big fashion store chains? However he does it, leave them subconsciously hooked by the thought of the new Valence product. Buy it in quantity, display it everywhere, implant the idea of its quality into the subconscious of the sales force. Like the way we went through that special showroom project last May.'

'Face cream? He may find the assignment a bit beneath him. He has his choosy moments, you know.'

'It's a challenge. He usually enjoys that.'

'Patrick,' said Hugo stiffly, 'is not a circus performer.'

Dr. Lanner was a parapsychologist who had devoted most of his adult life to investigating paranormal phenomena from a clinic in Austria, meeting or carrying on lengthy correspondence with fellow researchers in the field of telepathy, psychic phenomena, prediction and dream interpretation. It was in Salzburg that he had met the young widow of the latest generation to own Burntrigg estate. She was on a protracted holiday, reluctant to go back to her empty house, and in addition had been advised to take a long rest cure because of her physical problems — an increasing arrythmia spasmodically disturbing her heart. When she did return, it was with Lanner as her husband.

She helped him establish his own research

centre in the Hall. Ruth suspected, and had heard local gossip on the same lines, that little intensive work got done. Lanner dabbled, continued to indulge in correspondence with fellow devotees of the occult and preternatural, and published some highly contentious pamphlets designed for limited circulation.

When his wife died he was faced with the fact that their estate was insolvent. He had no talent for putting it back on its feet in any normal businesslike way. It was through Matthew Armour that he had been able to do a deal to let the premises profitably to Copsholm Communications, and it was with Matthew's mystified assistance that he had introduced an unusual practitioner into their promotional activities.

Having tracked down and seized — or, as he preferred to put it, rescued — Patrick Robson, Hugo Lanner tried keeping the boy very much under his own control. Occasionally he let fall hints of knowing how dangerous 'the others' were, though never explaining in full to Ruth or her partner who these others might be.

Sometimes he would talk expansively about the young man's incredible gift. At other times he could be dourly uncommunicative, as if determined that nobody should usurp his own authority. To him, Patrick's life here was an experiment, keeping the young man occupied and testing his resources while the rigorously academic Dr. Lanner made notes for some thesis to be published in due course.

In spite of his remark about circus acts, Ruth more than once saw him as a ringmaster, with Patrick as his star performer — indeed, his only performer. She was fairly confident that he could not do without her and the Copsholm team. They were all part of his experiment, and he doubtless felt they should be grateful for being allowed to take part.

'One of the interesting things that the young man's proud of,' he said, 'is that he was born at midnight on a Midsummer's Day.' It was one of those little titbits of information he occasionally allowed himself to impart. 'I am inclined to think that he may believe this might go some way to make up for the mismatch of his parents.'

'Mismatch?'

'My researches have traced the blood-line way, way back. There has always been this race of seers, gifted with what some have loosely called second sight, taking in clairvoyance, and a talent for divination and the interpretation of dreams. The 'Gifted Ones.' Some were respected by ancient communities and set aside for special care and further secret initiations by their . . . their *mentors*. Sometimes they were fawned on, appealed to, begged for help. But then, just as often they were persecuted, burnt as witches or stoned to death. Even today they keep a low profile. And the ability to motivate people while asleep, far beyond the tricks of stage hypnotists, has been kept a secret for a long, long time.'

'It's still a bit creepy,' said Ruth. 'I've always thought my dreams were my own subconscious blunderings. Can't say I'd be keen on having them manipulated by somebody else. Not that Patrick has ever actually eavesdropped on me — not as far as I know.'

Hugo seemed in expansive mood.

'Jung's theory of each human being as an island, separate on the surface but joined to each other below by the earth, includes the importance of the ability to dream. Are we in nightly communication just with our own unconscious selves, or are there wider communications? And those who over the centuries have preserved the gift of tuning in to them?' He leaned forward, which made his abnormally long chin cast a deep shadow on his neck. 'We're lucky,' he intoned, 'to have got our hands on such a gifted one, even if he's slightly flawed.'

'Flawed?'

'That mixed parentage. His mother was in the direct bloodline of the seers, but she married out with the kindred. An ordinary run-of-the-mill man, in a run-of-the-mill relationship. Love,' sighed Hugo. 'Sexual desire. And a desire for . . . well, *ordinariness*. I've come across plenty of examples of that in my studies. Like the old legends of a fairy or a selkie marrying a mortal. What sort of offspring can they expect? But Patrick does seem to be overcoming his inbred disadvantages.

Doing very well indeed.'

Under my tutelage. The words went unspoken.

Ruth said: 'What happened to them — his father, and the mother?'

Early in their relationship she had gathered that Hugo and Matthew had rescued the boy from some danger that was always blurred over. She was left with a vague picture of something on the lines of the stories one read in the newspapers of brutal treatment in an orphanage or broken home. Matthew had always been reluctant to speak about it, as if he had been inveigled into something unsavoury, in spite of the financial rewards. He certainly resented Hugo virtually taking over their joint captive.

'The father disappeared,' said Hugo now. 'The mother was out when . . . when the boy was in danger. When, thank heavens, we got our hands on him.'

'Shouldn't it worry us' — she voiced a doubt that kept coming back to nag at her — 'this spying on other people's dreams? And trying to . . . well . . . *twist* them?'

Hugo stiffened. 'You getting squeamish?'

'Of course not, but — '

'Not as long as the profits roll in?' he said silkily.

'The mother. She's never shown up since? Never tried . . . '

'It's been up to him to establish contact if he wanted to. They share the same gift.'

'And he hasn't done anything to trace her? Or . . . listen for her?'

'I'm not sure it would be good for the boy to have her back.'

'She might not like the way we're using his talents?'

'He might be distracted. Not trusting her, after she left him alone. And we don't want him distracted, do we?' Hugo drew his legs in and folded his arms. 'Don't get too worried about the methods, any more than you'd worry about the ability to punch an equation into a computer and wait for it to come up with the answer. Think of the electronic cyber attacks that shake up computers and networks, jamming or injecting with a virus. Just what Patrick can do with human dreams — beaming in sly suggestions or instructions so subtly that nobody's aware of being leaned on.'

'And you're worrying about *him* being leaned on — by us? Used too intensely?'

'I promise you I'll take good care of that. He's too valuable to let him burn out too soon, after all I've put into him.'

'An investment?'

'Not just financial. I'm privileged to be watching over the development of his genius.'

'Genius?'

'What else would you call it?'

Ruth became more businesslike. 'Hadn't we better get round to consulting him on this current matter? That *is* what we're here for today. What *he's* here for.'

'I think we could bring him into the picture now,' said Hugo magnanimously. 'Shall I call him down?'

Part Two

NOCTURNES

1

So there'll come a time when I'm dead and they think that'll be the end of me. Pathetic, all of them. There is so much more to come. I'll not be left to rot in the ground like the rest. No one shall decree my death.

The shadow, though, is growing insolently darker. For years it has taunted me on the edge of my dreams. At first just a vague grey haze, but as time went on it began to grow slowly more substantial. Sometimes I've fancied it was threatening, though it's never made a move towards me. Or it might simply be a sentry, a guardian of some kind. When is it finally going to turn and look straight at me?

It was certainly not watchful or protective when the accident happened and my leg got smashed up and so many things became different and difficult. I ought to have been better at foreseeing trouble myself; but I didn't yet know the full strength of my own talents. Not until I was suddenly taken away from that boarding school and was seeking consolation in dreams did a new world open up to make up for the drabness of the daytime hours.

'It's not natural for him,' I heard my father say to my mother one evening, soon after the move. But if he felt the same as I did, why had he let it happen?

The big grey building was a residential school endowed for the sons of war veterans. My father, I gathered, had been invalided out after a spell in somewhere he would never talk about. He was an IT expert, living on the school premises and looking after a lot of technical stuff, as well as teaching classes for some of the older boys. My mother was the cook.

But did that mean I had to be there all the time too? If so, why couldn't I live with them in their school flat, where I was only allowed to have supper on Saturdays and Sundays, instead of sleeping in a dormitory with five other boys? I didn't much like any of them, and one was particularly creepy: a thin-faced boy with a way of sneering at anyone he'd decided to pick on that twisted the corners of his mouth into a drooping grin. He was always watching you, as if to decide when would be a good time to spit at you.

I tried to steer clear of those sneers in the daytime. But at night he began to taunt me.

What had kept me going since coming to this special school were my dreams. That was where reality lay. They were more vivid than anything in the daylight hours. I was able to decide exactly where I wanted to go and how I wanted to spend my time. I visited fields I had never known before, and strolled along the edges of a river or through a garden of beautiful flowers. Anybody I encountered turned out to be a friend, and we played games I rarely remembered when I woke up. All that was left was a delightful glow, which faded during the dismal procession of lessons and study periods and supposedly healthy physical training. But night would come again, and I would choose which direction to take.

Until Dominic Lynch slid into my dreamworld.

Dormitory lights had gone out. One boy was sniffling a bit before going to sleep. I waited patiently for the moment to leave my bed for somewhere remote yet far more substantial, gradually drawing me in and then making me free of its whole shimmering landscape. Tonight I knew at once that there was an intruder. The usual shadow was there, silent and motionless just off the corner of my eye; but there was another figure, blocking my path. I felt rather than heard Dominic sniggering, and tried to walk off in another direction.

'Come here often, Robson?'

All at once we were no longer in my favourite patch of woodland, but on the edge of a busy road with a lot of cars whizzing up and down, and a lot of dust blowing up into our faces.

I said: 'Get out of here. I don't want you here.'

'Too bad. You've got a lot to learn, young Patrick.'

I willed him to disappear. It was a weird sensation, trying to thrust him away out of my dream — not with my hands, but with my mind. He sensed what I was doing. He had been expecting it, and was ready with what felt like a tight band round my head, tightening as if to hold me still.

'Go away. Just . . . go . . . away.' The words were thick in my throat.

'It's all part of the training, Patrick. You have to learn who's boss. And then maybe they'll let you practise the real tough stuff. If *you're* tough enough.' The sneer was in every word as well as in his narrow, warped face.

What was he talking about? I was confused. I couldn't be sure whether I was dreaming about Dominic or *he* was dreaming about *me*. Was he invading my dream, or luring me into his?

I had to throw him back into his own world. I put all my effort into it, straining my head as if I could make it swell outwards and split that band squeezing tighter and tighter. And I found I could do it. Gradually I was weakening the grip he had on me. He glared, trying to hold me there, but his face began to dissolve, and bit by bit the rush of traffic behind him was dissolving too, and gradually trees and hedges were shaping themselves all around us.

With one last heave I threw him out.

Next day we passed in the playground, and he turned to glare at me; but I grinned back, and he didn't stop to argue or try anything on with me.

So we both possessed what must surely be an unusual gift. Or was it normal, something I would find everybody had developed by the time they grew up?

Or something special about this school?

It wasn't just that I was dreaming things so vividly: I was hearing things, too. One of the few school subjects I enjoyed was music. It didn't seem to belong in the same world as the maths and electronics and supposedly practical matters, and something they called history, which featured an awful lot of stuff about modern terrorism and counter-terrorism. Why all that was supposed to be important to us I couldn't think. But music was real and important. It meant hours of lovely reverberations inside my head, and all through my body. I remember being jolted wide-awake in the middle of a lesson when the visiting music teacher played some piano pieces by a composer called Bartók. At the time I didn't grasp what a composer was. The music existed all on its own, for my benefit, without anyone being responsible for putting it all together. And the night after first hearing that very special piece, I carried it with me into blissful sleep and *saw* it as well: spiky, in sharp colours, fencing with itself . . .

Our Headmaster could surely know nothing about these things infiltrating my dreams. But he was always watchful, always consulting members of his staff, and doing what I supposed were his own sort of sums.

'You feel a special interest in music, Robson?'

He looked at me across the heads of others in the class.

'I like some of it, yes, sir.' It was a safe enough answer.

'We'll have to see how it ties in with any of your particular talents. Mustn't let it go to waste.'

Somebody sniggered. I knew it was Dominic Lynch.

And then there was that visiting group who came to give two recitals in the school hall. There was a man playing what he told us was a clarinet, a young woman with a flute, and four other middle-aged women playing some stringed instruments.

It was a wonderful afternoon. Even more wonderful was my dream that night.

I had gone wandering, as I often did, waiting for some response from somebody or something, and found myself in the head of the clarinettist. In sleep he was still playing to himself one of the pieces we had heard earlier. And I not only heard the notes but felt the keys beneath my fingers, and an exciting tingle in my teeth as certain notes vibrated up the instrument. It was in A major: that I knew without knowing what the phrase meant. On the top A or the C# below, the sizzling feeling went right up to the top of my skull.

But then he changed key. The sounds were mellower, the feeling now was just a faint throb between my lips. I wasn't ready for it. I plunged into his mind, demanding that he go back to what he'd been playing before, trying to re-create the vibrations in his head. Bewildered, he twitched about in bed, trying to cancel me out. But I persisted.

Until he woke up, and I had lost him.

The group's performance the next day wasn't a patch on their first one. The first violinist kept glancing at the clarinettist after he had produced a series of squeaks and sudden squawks like the honking of a goose.

How did I know that, when I had never seen or heard a goose? What store of knowledge had I been dipping into without consciously willing it?

After the recital, the Headmaster made a short speech of thanks, the usual boring stuff, and we all clapped, and I caught Dominic staring at me in a questioning sort of way.

Only as were leaving the hall did I sense that the Headmaster was looking at me too, with very much the same expression. I tried to walk briskly past him, but he stepped across my path.

'Ah, Patrick,' he said amiably. 'Last

night you had a dream?'

It was a statement, not an accusation. And he had switched from my surname to my Christian name, which was unusual when addressing any of us boys. But I wasn't going to let him in on my secret world. 'I don't know, sir. I . . . don't remember. Not specially.'

But he could see I remembered. He might have been watching me while I was watching the clarinettist get things wrong. Yet he didn't scold me, or punish me for not owning up. In fact he looked rather pleased.

He and one of the other teachers seemed to be watching me all the time from then on, especially first thing in the morning, as if to detect signs of any other dream goings-on. What had it got to do with school and lessons and all that; and how did they guess?

So many questions, and as a boy only just approaching his teens I was afraid to ask. Anything I learned would have to be by my own methods.

Such as why Dominic Lynch and I were considered slightly different from the rest of the pupils. Because I was beginning to suspect that we were being thrown together — being groomed for something special. *Groomed* . . . another of so many words and ideas that came drifting into my mind without being asked for; and not fully understood.

Things came to a head on the day we were all sent out on a day's physical training in the local woods.

In fine weather we had often been taken for walks there in small groups, guarded at the sides by teachers as if there was a danger of somebody grabbing one of us and running off. Were we all being trained as cadets and then as soldiers, only a special kind of soldier? I had enjoyed those woods much more when I revisited one particular corner in dreams. Yet this particular morning I felt uneasy, with a lingering echo of something that had worried me in dreams the night before — something that had somehow been *planted* in my mind.

This time we weren't just walking in strictly organized groups at a fixed pace, but divided into groups to do a lot of physical jerks, bending and stretching, and swinging rhythmically from tree branches which had been carefully chosen for safety.

Whether it was deliberate or purely by chance was hard to tell, but after the first twenty minutes Dominic and I found ourselves on our own in a small clearing: alone together, that is, unless you counted a couple of shadows flitting behind the trees on the shadowy side of the clearing. Not my familiar night shadow, but ordinary human beings, watching, waiting for something we were supposed to give them.

Mr. Snelling, one of the masters, sauntered out of the green shade for a moment, far more casual than he ever was in the classroom.

'Getting ready for a duel?' he laughed. He didn't often laugh, and it didn't sound right. 'Only without swords or pistols, hey?'

They were growing impatient. I could have told them that any worthwhile clash between Dominic Lynch and myself could take place only in dreams.

All at once Mr. Snelling said: 'Tell you what, lads. It's a hot day. Let's all have a bit of a snooze, hey?'

So they did know. Of course they must have known all along. And knew who to choose.

I lay back on the tangy-smelling grass, and heard a rustle as Dominic did the same. Also I heard Mr. Snelling's footsteps squeaking away to the edge of the clearing and maybe beyond.

The warmth and scents and the glow of sunshine through my closed eyelids were lulling me into a state of readiness for some new and rewarding experience.

Only then, without opening my eyes, I saw Dominic standing above me. His voice reached into my head although his lips weren't moving. We were both half asleep, half aware of the other, groping out to strengthen the tie.

I heard him say 'You'd never have the guts, of course.'

'What are you talking about?' My own voice was slurred. I tried to sit up, although I'd sooner have gone off to sleep, a deeper sleep, away from the lot of them.

'That tree over there. Why d'you think they've taken the younger kids off into the woods? So they can go climbing. Proper climbing. You've been dumped here, because they know you're not up to it.'

'And what about *you*, then?' My voice was still strangled and reluctant. I didn't want to haul myself back up into wakefulness. And wasn't he putting all his weight into holding me down? 'You're here, like me.'

'To keep an eye on you. Stop you doing anything stupid. Only they don't realize just how stupid you are, do they?'

The challenge began to take on a shape. Shielding my eyes from the sun, though I wasn't conscious of moving my hand that way, I lumbered to my feet. Only inches away from me was the tree with long, sinuous branches that curled down and around at shoulder level.

'Don't risk it,' taunted Dominic. 'I'm telling you, you can't do it.' He raised his voice. 'You're not to try it, Robson. D'you hear me?'

I felt myself clawing at the nearest branch, finding it too weak and wobbly, reaching for anything, hauling myself up by a stronger branch, getting my right leg over and bracing myself to reach up and drag myself higher.

Then I came wide-awake and looked down.

I was too high up. Far too high for me. And deep inside the swirling within my head was Dominic Lynch's laugh, and he was saying so that only I could hear him: 'What are you going to do now?'

Mr. Snelling's voice was suddenly loud: 'You bloody fool, Robson!'

Then it became slow and measured. 'Listen, lad. Stay very still. Don't move until I tell you. Very still now . . . '

To which Dominic was suddenly adding with calculated clarity: 'I told you, Robson. I did tell you not to . . . '

And then I was falling.

* * *

I woke in a different room from the usual dormitory, in a different bed. As my eyes opened, a woman's voice called, and within a matter of minutes there were three or four people leaning over me. An awful racking pain clawed its way up my left leg — or what remained of it.

'Suggest another dose of . . . '

'That last injection, doctor . . . '

'And how are we feeling today, young man?'

I was in hospital. I didn't know anything about hospitals, but somehow it felt like school only more military. All I knew about things military were fragments I had picked up from my father, and those were very muddled. But there did seem a strictness about it all rather than any gentle care and encouragement. I sort of guessed it was all part of the same lot of buildings as the school. Like a barracks, I thought, whatever a barracks was . . . or were.

Somebody tried to tell me what had happened to me and what they had done about it. Something about an anaesthetic, which meant 'We put you to sleep for a little while.' I didn't recall any dreams from that sleep. Then a man with grey hair and pebbled spectacles sat on the edge of my bed and explained that I had shattered my left leg so badly it had been necessary to amputate it below the calf.

'In the old days,' he said in an odd mixture of solemnity and cheerfulness, 'you would have been severely crippled. As it is, after a few months we should be able to fit you with a nice, neat prosthesis, and you'll learn how to walk again.'

And I was supposed to think that this made me lucky, with nothing much to complain about?

At least I had this special room of my own now, and my mother and father were allowed to come and see me in the evenings. My mother was close to crying each time. 'They should never have allowed it to happen.'

My father was grim-faced. 'We should never have let them get their hands on him in the first place.'

But then they made a big thing of telling me the same sort of thing the doctor, or surgeon or whatever, had told me, and how lots of young men managed with only one leg. There were ways of fitting me with something, I'd be told all about it and given lots of exercises when they had assessed my condition, I was just to be patient.

Maybe I was expected to show myself as my heroic father's courageous young son. I'd been severely wounded, it hurt dreadfully, and I was expected to grin and bear it.

Hardest of all things to bear, Dominic was sent in to visit me regularly, bringing my supper before he went to get his own. It was difficult to tell whether this was meant as a punishment for his part in my so-called accident, or whether it was an attempt to draw us together. As far as I could make out from snatches of conversation between the staff, no disciplinary action had been taken against him other than what they regarded, I think, as 'a good talking-to'. They must surely have sensed the bitterness behind his forced smile. Inside I could tell he was gloating.

I forced myself to be polite, but only just, and each time waited impatiently for night and sleep and what awaited me. Among other things, there had to be a reckoning one day, somehow, with Dominic Lynch.

The Headmaster paid an early visit, just at the end of an hour when my mother and father had been visiting.

'Bearing up, Robson?' He had gone back to my surname. He was just as crisp when he turned to my parents. 'Making good progress, isn't he? A credit to you, Mr. Robson . . . Mrs. Robson.'

My father found difficulty in speaking to him, but had to make the effort because, I supposed, he had to keep his job in the school. Even so, though he kept his voice level and respectful, the anger was there. 'That should never have been allowed to happen.'

'It was an unfortunate accident, Mr. Robson. We regret it. But you know yourself how things can go wrong during a training session.'

'He was never meant for this sort of thing. That wasn't what we were promised.'

'On the contrary, Mr. Robson, you were assured of a very special future for him after he had gone through our highly specialized guidance.' He nodded smugly at my mother, as if they shared a very special secret together. 'It's a quite exceptional family trait, isn't it, Mrs. Robson? One not to be wasted.'

'For all the good it'll be to him now,' said my father.

'He still has great potential.'

'In that state?'

'I think Mrs. Robson understands.'

My father made sure that the Headmaster had left before giving my shoulder an awkward squeeze and taking my mother's arm to lead her away. I was left to wonder what my mother understood that my father failed to grasp.

The night world now grew even more enchanting. I no longer waited for pictures to drift into my dreams, or force their way in, but decided to go hunting — not just luring ideas of other people into my dreams but tracking them down in their own dreams. Bedridden, I was a prisoner in the daytime world, or else just the subject of long hours of exercises on my leg, injections, and transfers to and from a wheelchair which I had to drive round and round the edge of a gymnasium with my fingers gripping the wheels and my arms thrusting and dragging back, on and on. But night time, which had always offered a release, now opened up wider and wider as my only real world whatsoever.

I was so keen to explore all this that often I couldn't get to sleep. Tired by exercise and a brawny young woman's manipulation of my injured leg, I would lie there twitching, trying to force my mind away from the stabs of pain in that leg, visualizing what I might do, fuming with impatience. Until at last sheer physical weariness would win, and my eyes closed and I could begin to see clearly.

It's hard to explain how, crippled as I was physically, I had become mentally so much stronger. As if to compensate for my new disability, I was being granted another, richer talent. My mind had acquired the ability to float weightlessly out from me, sending out a signal and waiting for it to strike a response. Like radio signals and tuned circuits and . . . but where did I get even a glimmering of such a comparison? That was my father's field of activity. Somehow I must have snatched a few shreds of it from his mind without either of us being aware of it at the time. But anyway, I relaxed, and drifted, until I could feel myself being drawn almost magnetically towards my target. Or my prey, the way I saw it.

And I set my sights on Dominic Lynch. I could not wound him physically; but if I could find a point where he might be vulnerable, if I could just pick up the right signal, the note that would ring true . . .

Came the evening when he had brought my supper and set it on the wheeled table swung across the bedclothes. Then he looked down and made a funny little whimpering noise.

I pretended not to notice as he wriggled round the far side of my bed towards the door, keeping his hands on the counterpane and shoving his feet out at an angle, sprawling as far away as he could get them. It was an awkward manoeuvre, and it was only by edging my head a bit up the pillow that I could get at an angle enabling me to see down to a patch of the floor.

A large spider had darted out from under the bed and was now sitting there, utterly still, but looking as if its next move might be towards the door.

Dominic gulped, pushed himself upright, said 'Goodnight then, Robson', and stumbled out into the corridor.

Spiders! He was terrified of spiders!

That night I sank contentedly into sleep and went in search of him. For a time I was frustrated by the fact that he was still awake. I tried hard not to get too impatient, which might wake me up and spoil things.

At last there came something like the tug of a string in my mind, and I knew he had fallen asleep. It was now only a matter of holding on to that invisible string and hauling myself along it until I was in his world.

Dominic was relaxing in the middle of a little park, which bore a resemblance to one corner of the woodland where we'd been taken for that so-called physical training. He had somehow acquired a little dog, and kept throwing sticks for it to fetch. Any time it hesitated, or dropped the stick halfway back, he kicked it or smacked it hard across the face. Then he'd make silly slobbering noises over it.

I took a deep breath, tense and ready. He felt it as he might have felt a puff of wind across the grass, and looked round uneasily. Then he made a big effort to shrug it off and go back to the dog.

Until the park suddenly closed in all round him. I'd made it contract into a tight little square with a closely packed hedge all round. And a spider as large as a thrush sat on top of one bit of hedge and I was forcing Dominic to expect it to fly at him.

He stood still, frozen, for what seemed an eternity. I could feel his heart beating, and a sour taste rising in his throat. Then he made a dash for the opposite side of the square, looking for a way to get out. But there was no gate; no gap. Instead, a flurry of spiders came seething up out of the leaves, and sprayed over him, dancing on his hair, scuttling down his shoulders and inside the blue shirt he was wearing. He began tearing at his collar. The spiders flowed down his arm and out of his cuffs. He began trying to shout but couldn't squeeze a sound out.

Then it was as if he could see me staring

at him over the hedge. He forced himself to glare back, trying to drive me out of his dream; but I put all my effort into it, and the spiders swirled around him as thick and dizzying as a cloud of midges.

He turned and ran. But there was no way out from where I had penned him in. No way except by clawing himself upwards, up and away and out of his dream, waking up in the dormitory and sobbing to himself until the boy nearest to him woke up as well and in the distance, fading swiftly, I heard him grumbling 'Shut up, Lynch, what's got into you?'

At breakfast the Headmaster dropped in to see me. He gave me a long, knowing look, and an approving smile.

'Sleeping well, Robson? Not kept awake by any discomforts?'

'I'm fine, sir.'

'Good lad.'

That was all. I couldn't tell whether he was hoping for a confession, or was pleased enough by what he knew or guessed.

I went through a long, wearying programme of physical exercises to strengthen my one good leg and make the remains of the other as supple as possible. Weeks passed as I exercised numbly, waiting for night and a world in which I moved freely, with no concept of being crippled.

Something else I had to try. I had to follow up my attack on Dominic's mind with a more ambitious one. Could I reach out in sleep and find out what the Headmaster himself was dreaming — or afraid of dreaming?

It took three nights before I made contact. And then it was very confused. He was different, older than me, and on what I can only say, in language I had only vaguely acquired, a different wavelength. But I caught a glimmering of his restlessness, then of recognition, and felt I had better run away quickly.

At his next visit to the hospital wing he smiled another of those knowing smiles at me. Later in the day I heard him talking to someone in a doorway some yards off, his voice with that quiet but carrying resonance you get in school and hospital corridors.

'Yes, he's undoubtedly one of them. The power's there.'

'That and the music. They do complement each other.'

'Yes, the two elements. In harmony, as you say. We'd better notify the trustees.'

I hadn't been sure whether I ought to tell my father and mother about my dreams. But then it seeped into my mind that my mother knew anyway. Her glances at me, sort of sideways on, half affectionate and half worried, were quite different from the Headmaster's watchfulness; but she *knew*.

I overheard them, too, after one visit when they thought they were out of earshot.

'You can guess what they're planning.' It was my father, gruff and at the same time plaintive. 'All this talk of a new course. This is what they've been after all along.'

'It could be for his own good. We've always been told that the sort of training he'll get — '

'Training for what? All that gabble about — I mean, for Christ's sake — 'expanding his parameters'. Now there'll be no stopping them. Or him.'

'Malcolm, my love, he's . . . *gifted*. A very special talent. He can't help that. You knew when you married me that it was always . . . well, a possibility. It's been there right down through our family. And you did know when we had him that the gift might come through with him.'

'Gift? A curse, more like.' His harsh sigh was like a gust of wind. 'If only I hadn't let myself be dragged into this job. I should have had the guts to say no.' A door opened and their voices faded. I couldn't tell which of them said, 'Maybe it's not too late.'

It was only a week after this that they took me away from the school.

★ ★ ★

All three of us left very quickly, without explaining. Not to me, anyway. Nor could I find out what they might have told the school authorities. I tried asking, but was told I was too young to understand but that everything would be all right. All I remember was being hustled out of the place into a car late one evening, as if we were criminals making a getaway. Not that I knew about criminals and getaways at the time: only looking back can I express it that way.

The very first night after we had moved, I tried to use my talents in plucking the truth out of my father's dreams, but could find only a confusion of ideas and what sounded like self-excuses, until abruptly the vision was wiped out like a television screen going suddenly blank.

Again that had to be my mother's doing. I was sure of it. Whatever strange talent I had, it was inherited from her. And she had the power to close a door against me.

But there would be other people, lots of other people, who didn't have that power. They were waiting out there for me, none of them knowing I was coming.

One thing had followed us from those nights in the school dormitory. Or was there ahead of us, waiting for me. That dark, watchful shape was in its usual corner of the night. Still not showing a face or even a properly filled-out body. Just a mistiness that might without any obvious warning grow as solid and meaningful as the furniture, my parents . . . as myself, even.

2

For me there was now just a room in a
house of our own, and my mother and
father assured me that I wouldn't have to
mix with other people again until
. . . well, until what?

'You're very special,' my mother said in
a loving yet somehow a bit scared voice.
'When you're ready, you'll understand.' I
remember that repeated nod of hers, like
a little bird, and her insistent little voice.
'We're safe here.' I could sense that she
was insisting on something to herself as
much as to me.

Now that my father no longer had
maintenance work to do in the school, or
boys to teach occasionally, he began
spending a lot of time shut away with his
computer. I knew he had to make money
for us to live on. But the work didn't
make him happy. Perhaps as a war hero
he resented having a son whose accident
had made it impossible for him ever to

follow in that tradition; and resented having to work in order to pay for my upkeep.

Once I overheard him squeezing words out at my mother. 'This place *isn't* safe, you know. Sooner or later — '

'We have to be patient.' There was such a loving note in her voice. I knew, without knowing exactly what it was like to be in love, that she loved him very much. It ought to have been warming, embracing me as well. But sometimes I sensed there was something waiting to crack.

Father had never smoked in school that I could remember. Nobody did. But he was doing so now. It gave a faint yellow tinge to the edge of his bristly moustache, which curled at one end to cover part of the deep scar which ran down his left cheek from above his ear, as if that bit of his face had been dragged open and then jammed clumsily together again.

The house was a single-storey building with some narrow doorways and awkward corners that made it difficult for me to manoeuvre my wheelchair — no prosthetic leg for me, having been removed from hospital before the time for that had come. I soon found it less trouble just to stay in my own room at the end of the building. It had one window overlooking what I supposed was a small yard of some kind. I couldn't see out: some sort of mesh had been put over the glass, either to stop anybody peeping in or to stop me looking out, or both.

What saved the room from being dark was a large window in the sloping roof, at an angle above my bed. I used to slide along a curved board from my wheelchair onto my bed and lie there getting my breath back, staring up each time through glass that in this case was not covered with anything. Sometimes a bird flew over, or there were interesting changes in the sky — brightness one minute, then a drift of cloud pouring shadows over the edge of the window frame. Occasionally on a warm day my mother would prop the window open with a bit of serrated metal, and then the colours were sharper.

Now that she was no longer fully occupied with cooking in the school, my mother had time on her hands. She began reading to me a lot, which I soon realized was more for her benefit than mine: I could perfectly well read any of the books which they had brought with them or which they picked up for me in what they called second-hand shops — a description which for some reason made my father look sullen again — but it helped her to relax, and she must have felt she was in some way contributing to my education and general well-being.

Perhaps things would become clearer if we could all three share more.

One breakfast I decided to tell them about a dream I'd had, to see what reactions I'd get.

I'd been wandering on a hillside without any reason I could think of for being there. It was just that it was an agreeable place, which I had conjured up for myself, and in sleep I suffered no restrictions: I could walk freely, with both legs working normally. But on this occasion, without going more than a few steps I found myself stuck in some mud. First my left foot was trapped, then I couldn't drag the right one forward.

'And then you were there, Dad,' I said across the table at him, 'and I wanted you to lift me up so I could get close to the stream and wash the mud off.'

My mother laughed an uneasy laugh. 'What a funny old dream. And I'll bet Dad hoisted you up in a flash and carried you off.'

'Well, no.'

My father tried to laugh as well, but it came out awkwardly. 'Oh, nothing ever goes right in dreams.'

'No, because there were these two men.'

They didn't move, yet I felt them both go stiff inside.

'Two men' — the dream picture was slipping away, the way most dreams do the moment you wake up, yet this bit hung on in my mind — 'just seemed to be there, watching you . . . and then watching *me*. As if they wanted to get closer to me and talk to me, but you were in the way.'

'No. Oh, no.' It was no more than a whisper.

'Well, that's enough of that nonsense.'

My mother was on her feet, clearing the table, making a lot of noise as she loaded the dishwasher. 'You'll have lots and lots of silly dreams, like we all do. Mustn't let them upset you.'

And next night I did indeed have another. Only this time there was no sign of my father. Somehow I knew he had been kept out of it. By my mother? Or by them — the two men, their faces and bodies becoming a lot clearer this time?

Those faces were determined, gleeful, pleased as if they had found something very special. As if they recognized me as what they'd been searching for and wanted to get their hands on me for . . . well, for what?

I didn't want to know them.

But they kept coming, steadily getting larger. I was shivering, wanting to turn and get away, force myself to wake up out of my dream. But my feet were stuck again, worse than ever this time. This was *my* dream, and I ought to be able to take charge and leave it when I wasn't satisfied. But all I could do was shout — shout first into one man's face, then into the other's. I wasn't using words, just making a noise, which I couldn't understand myself.

They went on staring at me, their faces greedy and quite determined.

I *had* to show them they didn't belong. This was *my* dream, not theirs . . .

My feet came free at last. I reached out with my arms, pushing my way through a curtain, which was the only way out on to the hills again. It wouldn't give way. I was trapped in it, choking in its folds . . . and then I was awake and kicking the bedclothes off.

My father stared at me at breakfast. Was he upset at having been elbowed out of the way? But the dream was fading anyway, and this time I wasn't going to say anything.

When I was wheeling myself back to my room, before I could steer carefully round the door and close it, I heard him talking in an explosive sort of way, as if unable to keep the words in any longer. 'I knew they'd catch up sooner or later.'

'It was only a dream. They weren't real, they — '

'You knew they'd come looking for him. How in God's name do we keep him clear, now they've got through?'

'Just that once, it may mean nothing.'

'Last night — '

'We don't know anything happened last night. He hasn't said anything.'

'He didn't have to. *You* could tell. I know you could. It's in your blood. That same blood, that whole damned — '

'My dear, that's not fair. How many more times . . . you knew the risks when you married me.'

'I didn't realize . . . ' He let out a choked sort of sob. As I closed my door quietly, I think my mother must have been putting her arms round him, as she often did with me. Or, rather, as she often *had* done in the past. Even though we were closer together nowadays than when we had all of us been at that school, she hugged me less — and, somehow, more warily, as if never sure what I might be capable of.

On the single floor of the house next to my room were my parents' bedroom, a bathroom and a lavatory. Tucked away behind them was a sitting room, which led straight into the kitchen. The sitting room had a very large window overlooked by some other people's windows from across a narrow street, and I wasn't allowed there except in the evenings when the curtains were drawn.

I didn't much enjoy evenings along there. My father let me see television programmes which he had chosen carefully, and which he could quite often switch off suddenly because he had decided there was something unsuitable for me. He was never relaxed, anyway. He would keep glancing at the curtains to make sure they were properly closed, and he seemed to be always waiting for somebody to knock at the door. I was sure that if anyone did, he would wheel me hurriedly back to my room before he'd let my mother answer the door.

It got so that I preferred to stay on my own. And my father obviously preferred it that way.

But what if somebody *had* come to the door? Apart from the postman or some delivery man, that is — and they didn't come very often. What was there to be worried about? Maybe somebody from the school, asking about my welfare, or insisting on taking me on one side and running me through one of those examinations we'd so often had. All so they could 'notify the trustees'.

'Couldn't you take me out for a walk?' I asked one day when the sun was hot on the roof and my mother had propped the upper window open. 'One of the boys used to push me out in my wheelchair when I was convalescing. They said it was good for me.'

Oddly enough, I had asked only out of curiosity rather than a really intense desire to get out in the open. And I had known that there would be an excuse, an evasion, and that repeated assurance that sooner or later I would understand and be grateful.

So it was back to my solitude. Back to the vertical lines on the wallpaper, enclosing a curly pattern like a long green stem, with pink roses at regular intervals; back with the green line of damp writhing across the ceiling, and the dark brown rug that had worn to a scuffed pale brown beside my bed.

My room had its one big cupboard and a bed, and beside the bed a small table with a smaller cupboard underneath it. I can still feel in my fingertips what it was like to reach down to the latch of the cupboard and open it — how it stuck slightly, and how my little finger would just go through the ornamental hole in the middle of the latch.

Within this confined space I had to do my exercises, which I'd started in hospital. My father helped me to start with, but he soon grew impatient and handed the task over to my mother. I could almost hear him saying 'What's the point?' But she persevered and stood over me while I stretched my right leg, then moved my crumpled left stump out and back, and she took hold of it and turned and twisted it to and fro, out and back, until everything ached horribly but was, she assured me, 'getting so much better every day'.

I didn't think she was aware of quite how adept I was becoming. I was learning how to ease my way across the room by pushing myself up in my chair with my arms, gripping the arm of it with my left hand while reaching out with my right hand to clutch at the edge of the bookcase and swing my full weight out on to it and gradually edge towards the far side of the room.

The bookshelf was not a very long one, and not very high, which was a help when I wanted to venture across the room. It held the few carefully chosen books I'd been given, and which my mother read to me with decreasing frequency. And on top of it there came at last what I had been waiting for, without knowing it: a radio.

★　★　★

I had talked a lot about music and asked why we couldn't go to concerts like the ones I had known at school. There must be some, somewhere out there. I sought out a few in my dreams, but it was difficult to find any performance where I could be in the audience in the middle of the night. I went foraging into the minds of any musicians I could reach, some fairly close but others distractingly far away and unsteady. I couldn't hope to get the full sensation of the actual music without hearing it live and clear in the daytime. So at last, grudgingly — another reluctant expense — my father bought me this small radio.

As an expert in such things, he fixed it on Radio 3 for the music I wanted, with no freedom to explore other stations and hear talks that he thought unsuitable. 'There's a lot that you might find disturbing.' And sometimes he would check in the daily paper or a weekly radio magazine to see if there were any plays on Radio 3 which, again, I 'might find disturbing'. Then he would use some sort of remote control to switch the set off.

He never understood that music itself could be disturbing. Excitingly so. I never wanted pieces that were cosy, melodies that would lull me to sleep. Sleep for me was the place where I was most alive, and I wanted music which would carry over at full volume, every element of it vivid and unbroken. Silly little tunes that I could hum as I walked along — yes, in dreams I was capable of walking more and more miles — were useless. I wanted composers to hold me in the grip of their fingernails, biting into me, causing exquisite pain.

Only for a long time I still couldn't grasp the idea of there being people who actually composed that music. Although I remembered the name of Bartók and gradually associated those of Berg and Webern with pieces I enjoyed, these were only terms of reference rather than the names of real people.

And in those night-time wanderings I found myself looking for another human being who would hear and feel the same resonances: someone with whom I would be in harmony, yet at the same time clashing and rejoicing in wild, tormenting discords.

My dreams were becoming more coherent. Not just the occasional venture into unknown territory, but a complete life, more intense and colourful than my drab day-after-day existence. In daylight I was what you might call half asleep. In my bed, when I was really asleep, the dreams became real and solid, and all the people around me were as three-dimensional as myself. For the first time some of my old school companions came into focus. I didn't recognize them at first, because of course they had grown older. They seemed to recognize me at once, though. As I walked doubtfully towards them, they didn't smile. They looked scared. Someone, something, must have warned them against having anything to do with me. What concocted explanation had they been given about my sudden disappearance?

And then, one night, the two men were there again. Only this time it was much worse.

They spoke to me one after the other, the first trying to sound friendly, the other threatening. They blamed me for not going to them and believing in them. How could they exist in my dream if I didn't want to believe in them? I tried hard to tell myself that they weren't there, but they refused to fade.

'Tell us where you are,' said the one with grey eyes and a polite but severe voice.

I squeezed words out. 'No, I can't.'

'We're coming for you.' The other one had a face that kept changing shape, but his eyes were fixed and staring at me. 'You can make it easier just by telling us where you're living right now.'

Coming for me? But how could they, if they didn't know where I was? I couldn't have told them even if I'd wanted to. And I didn't want to.

'There's nothing to be frightened of,' said the first man.

'Not if you come to meet us,' said the second man.

I wasn't going to make one step towards them. I wanted to deny that they existed. They were trespassing — where had I come across that word? — and I wanted them driven out.

But suddenly I was seeing . . . he was making me see . . . a stream of boiling tar trickling towards me, and trapped in it were the feet of a tiny child, crying for help, reaching out arms to me, while the tar moved steadily towards my own feet, which were stuck to the ground so that I couldn't lift them clear.

'You wouldn't want to spend every night watching things like this, now would you?'

'Tell us where you *are*.'

I couldn't breathe. Couldn't move. Some power outside myself was forcing my feet to stay embedded like that child's, waiting. It must be my own special curse, this hallucination of being bogged down.

My mother came to my rescue. How she knew what was happening, I couldn't imagine; but she pulled me back, and somehow managed to throw a screen between me and that awful vision. And I woke up, and I was sure that I heard the click of the door closing as she went out. It ought to have been soothing, the contentment of my mother coming to help me, driving my nightmares away. But it was different from being cuddled and told stories in the daytime, which I had outgrown anyway. This wasn't normal.

I couldn't have thought that whole

vision up myself. There was nothing in my own mind for me even to dream of anything like it.

Was it going to be like this every night? Was I losing my grip on my own manipulation of this dreamworld of sleep, which had become so important that now I couldn't escape from it, but now couldn't rely on it when I was there? To control, instead of being controlled: I had to reassert myself.

I didn't like to look at my mother at breakfast. And my father knew somehow that something had happened, and looked at her as if blaming her but not knowing how to express it.

I wondered if I dared make another attempt at peering into their own minds to find answers to a lot of questions they had kept dodging. If I concentrated hard enough in my sleep, could I edge past my mother and steal up on my father before she was aware of it? Shutting out everything and everybody to either side, aiming precisely, using all the skills I had learnt so far.

I didn't have to travel any great

distance. The surroundings were familiar. I was still at home. I had made my way along the corridor into my parents' bedroom, and slid into another of my father's dreams as smoothly as if I had lifted the sheet and slid into bed alongside him.

And suddenly I was terrified again.

I was surrounded by fire. There was a man tottering away from a blazing metal thing, which I knew was an armoured car. I must have seen magazine photographs of one or a TV programme. Flames sprang from the man's head. He threw himself on the ground and rolled over and over, screaming. And at the same time, all mixed in with it, was a picture of another man thrown back against a rock, with a swirl of dust about his shoulders. Then somebody was leaning over him, holding him down with one hand and stabbing away with a large sort of knife, stabbing into his eyes and gouging them out.

And another of those metal things was rolling towards me from the side, and when I turned to run I was knocked over and finished up on the ground, twitching to and fro, beating my head with my hands, howling for help that wasn't going to come. Until I forced myself up on to my knees, forced myself to crawl towards another shape that was writhing on the ground, spouting fire from his shoulders, and tried to get a grip on him and drag him clear.

And then both of us were trapped. The ground was soft underneath, pulling us down. Every slight movement took long, long minutes. Flame was raging closer. Who was in charge? Who was going to win? In a nightmare, who's going to be the stronger?

I fought to free the yelling, screaming man; and then we were groping our way along the edge of what I knew had to be a dream — a dream which I had to escape, forcing myself to shake it off and wake up.

In the morning I said: 'What does 'Afghanistan' mean?'

My father stared at me. He knew where I had been last night.

'What makes you ask that?' My mother's voice was at its sharpest and most accusing 'Wherever did you come across a word like that?'

'You were in awful pain.' So many dreams fade the moment you wake up, but shreds of this one still clung to my mind. 'But you went on. You had to help that man who was in an even worse state. What were you fighting over?'

My father let out a shaky laugh. 'What, indeed? Did it ever make any sense?' His hands were trembling so that he had to clasp them together to try and make them stop. I had seen him like this just once or twice before, but never as bad as this, never racked by such convulsions.

My mother burst out: 'You should be proud of your father. He was a hero. That's why that very special school — '

'No! Leave it!' my father snapped fiercely

'If it was so special, why did you take me away from it?' I blustered. 'Running away like that, as if we'd done something wrong. Or as if I'd — '

'There was nothing to be ashamed of.' My mother was sitting very upright. 'Just that the time had come . . . I mean, the school had done everything it could, and — '

'Endowed by a government secret agency.' My father's voice was shaking as rhythmically as his arms. How did a hero in wartime become such a sad, shivering person in peacetime?

I persisted: 'Then why did I have to leave?'

'I'm sure we've already told you. They just didn't have anything left to teach you. They were . . . well, let's just say they had certain limitations.' My mother became suddenly brisk. 'Right. Finished your toast? Time you went back to your reading. Or is it one of your music mornings?' She came out with me and at the door of my room said quietly: 'Patrick, you mustn't go in . . . in *there*. Darling, you really must stay out of your father's dreams.'

Before I could ask how much she knew, and how she knew it, and wasn't it time we talked it all over, she had gone back to be with him and talk to him in that special loving voice she had. I left the door open for a few minutes and heard her say: 'Malcolm, are you really sure we oughtn't to get in touch with . . . well, someone? A doctor. Someone who could see about getting that leg of his better? I mean, at least if we'd let the school doctor go on looking after him, they could have done so much for him — '

'*For* him?' he rasped. '*With* him.'

'If we tried to find some other doctor, a specialist — '

'And lead them straight to him? Word would get out.'

In this, anyway, I knew better than they did: knew that for us it was not a matter of physical movement that counted, but of evasions within dreams, learning how to dodge the tentacles with which *they* were groping out towards us — towards me especially — or how to summon up the strength to confront them. Whoever 'they' were, they were still waiting, somewhere. In my night world, without warning there would come a feeling of being followed, but then when I turned to look over my shoulder there was nothing. No immediate sense of fear . . . but unease. How long before they felt strong enough to attack again, and where would that attack come from?

★ ★ ★

Rather than wait like bait in a trap, I decided to become a hunter myself: the stalker, wandering through the nightworld to find someone whose dreams made them vulnerable . . . and enjoyable.

I came across a middle-aged married couple where the husband tried hopelessly to make love to a wife who was getting bored with his failures, and dreaming of a more virile lover. I fed the idea of that lover more and more forcibly into her mind until she began to believe in him, and went searching for him — awake and asleep, forever unfaithful from now on.

Not ready for that sort of thing yet, my mother had said. I was learning fast, growing up fast — growing up very fast, mentally.

There was a girl who I found amusing for a while. Her mind was wide open to create pictures on the ceiling of brawny young men coming to pleasure her. Her mind was also receptive to any ideas I chose to implant there.

It took almost a week before she began to fret, not about the sensuous ideas themselves but about where they were coming from. She began to believe she was being trailed by a stalker. She never saw him in daylight, couldn't say where he was coming from, but couldn't shake him off. Her current boyfriend grew impatient with her continual fretting about this obscure, haunting pursuer, telling her that it was 'All in your mind'.

Which of course it was. And in my mind too, until I grew bored. He, too, grew bored, so we both left her, sobbing and throwing herself about on the bed, trying hysterically to sort herself out while I went exploring elsewhere in the teeming night hours.

In dreamtime there was no sense of days, weeks, months or years passing. I learnt about the whole world outside from overhearing other people's interior world. I ceased to feel I was a prisoner. There was nothing I could experience by going outside that I couldn't conjure up here inside, learning night after night how much I could cope with, how to steer events the way I wanted them to go, making people dance to my tune.

One puzzling picture kept reappearing in my dream landscape. At first I thought it was just part of the scenery. But it showed up so often, as if it had some special meaning, that I didn't know whether to be irritated or comforted by its familiarity.

One afternoon when my father was busy in his own corner of the sitting room and my mother was fussing about my room, tidying it, I risked throwing the question at her, quite sure deep down that she would know the answer. 'What's that stone that I keep seeing?'

She gulped, and pretended for a moment or two not to have heard me. But she was growing more and more aware of what the two of us shared.

'It's a good luck stone,' she said. 'To keep evil away. And for handfasting.'

'Handfasting?'

'An old tradition of the Borders. A man

and a woman reach through the hole in the stone and hold hands while making a vow.'

'What's a vow?'

'A promise that has to be kept. They swear to live as handfast man and wife for one year from the date of their tryst. At the end of that year, if they still wish it, they will marry; or agree to part, without reproach.' And now her voice took on its usual off-putting tone. 'You're not ready for that sort of thing yet.'

I was becoming more and more certain that I was ready for anything.

So confident that when the two men reappeared in my dream later that week I didn't wait for them to come too close with their threats. I'd got a slight stomach ache after supper, and now wondered if it could be put to use. I tightened my whole being round it, intensifying and directing the pain at the first of the two men. It was like reaching a hand deep into his body, my fingers getting a grip on the lining of his stomach and squeezing, twisting it until he was doubled up, clutching his belly, screaming a silent scream right down the streets of the night. Then I made it worse for him by urging him to help in his own destruction. Trying not to obey, he was forced to thrust his own hand into his guts alongside mine, helping me to tug the twisted, steaming rope of his intestines out.

Then his whole body began dissolving into a thin, steaming vapour, his face collapsing in on itself and disappearing. The second man was fleeing into nothingness. I let him go, and awoke exhausted but aglow with fulfilment.

Later that day I was sitting close to my father when he switched on the television for the early evening news. There were reports on an earthquake somewhere, followed by the faces of some smug-looking men going in and out of Parliament. Then my father let out a sudden cry.

'That's our street, for God's sake.' He was staring wide-eyed at the screen. 'Only three or four blocks from here.'

The corpse of a man had been found lying on his side with his intestines spilling out on the pavement. They didn't

129

show the actual scene, but interviewed a police officer who said they were puzzled. It didn't look like a gang attack, didn't really look like an attack at all. 'As though he had exploded,' the newsreader summed up at the end. 'A medical report says that the man's whole stomach had burst from within.'

'That close to us,' my mother whispered, staring a question at me.

I hadn't let him get *too* close, I could have said to them. But I kept it contentedly to myself.

★   ★   ★

Many a night now I would lie awake for a long time, not because I was afraid of sleep but almost because I wanted to postpone the intensity of what waited for me. And then at last I would go out into the dreamworld where I was practising how to feel in charge of things.

And where I was beginning to educate myself through other people's dreams, more immediate and lasting than the books that father allowed me to read, and the television programmes he had allowed me to watch. Picking the brains of scholars and schoolmasters, soaking up an education from their subconscious. Not that I had known that word until now, but for a long time I had sensed the reality of it.

Sometimes the concepts were confusing. In their dreams, teachers and authors and businessmen were trying to relax from their daytime jobs. I had to step warily, picking and choosing, through a world that was more real than the drabness of daytime but still bewildering even as I grew older and more receptive.

More and more there came flashes of things I felt must be acutely significant. Again and again the shape of that stone — what my mother had called a handfasting stone — formed itself out of the shadows, dissolving just before I could reach it. I found myself visiting it without having willed it: walking towards it as if this was exactly what I had expected to be there, and then losing it again. Until one day it must solidify and stay there, challenging me. While at the same time there has been that other, less solid shape drifting like a wisp of fog at the edge of my vision. Inhaling something of me from deep down rather than simply watching. Measuring my performance, ready to criticize, the way the schoolmasters did — or, like them, hinting at an unspoken approval?

And was the time coming when I could challenge that silent watcher, making it turn and face me? And then there's that mysterious incantation. Impossible to tell whether the ghostly sentinel has found a voice, or whether these words have crept into my mind by some whim of my own, turning into a repetitive musical chant, echoing away into some dark infinity.

Sooner or later you will have to choose.

3

As I had grown older and taller I had discovered, in spite of the inadequacy of my incomplete left leg, how to look out of the skylight. It involved edging myself to the head of the bed and heaving my back up against the wall bit by bit until I could get a grip on the edge of the window frame. Having pushed the counterpane to one side I straightened my right leg, striving to keep it steady on the uncertain, slippery base of sheets while I eased the window up slot by slot on its long metal catch until I was able to peer down the roof into a far corner of the yard.

The street — if there was a street on that side of the house — was out of sight. Without risking hauling myself right up, my one good foot in the air, and clutching the frame desperately for no more than a few seconds, I could see no more than a limited area of that outside world. Above the far wall of our yard — I assumed it was ours — there was the blank end wall of a house much bigger than ours, rising to two storeys. Within the angle of the two walls below me were neat stacks of wood under a corrugated-iron roof, presumably for our sitting room fireplace.

The first time I dared to climb up and look out, I saw nobody. The second the same. Then the third time, in the middle of an afternoon, I held on to the window frame and watched two boys in the middle of the enclosed yard. How they got in, I couldn't see. They would hardly have come through the house — our house, which was never open to visitors. Out of sight there must be a door into the yard from the street. They ran to and fro across that sector of what to me was a foreign country. They looked small and distant, yet very clear. I felt I could reach out and pick them up.

'What the hell . . . ?'

It was my father's indignant shout. The boys scurried away out of sight. I heard the creak and slam of what must have been the door to the street. I kept my head well down, inside the frame.

Why hadn't I shouted to them and asked to be rescued? Once people knew I was here, my parents wouldn't be able to keep me shut up any longer. For that matter, I suppose it would have been possible to choose an unguarded moment when I could race my wheelchair along the passage to the front door and out into the street. Yet I had long ago lost that feeling of being imprisoned. The possibilities of the outside world were not as attractive as the lures of my interior world.

It was only a sort of detached curiosity that impelled me, late one evening after my parents had gone to bed, to heave myself up on to my wobbly perch. I eased the window open and looked out.

Moonlight made the roof silver. Everything had sharp edges: the gutter looked very close, and housetops some way away looked just as close. Shadows were very black, the moonlight very bright and clear. Some of the stacks of wood were twisted by those shadows into hunched shapes. You could think you saw things moving when they weren't.

Then I saw something that did move. I saw a shadow that wasn't a shadow. It crept across the bright patch and paused by one of the stacks. It was all black one moment, then it swung round and I saw that it had a face. Another moment, and it was joined by another shape; only this one was not so dark — its arms were bare and white, and there was a gleam along its hair.

A boy; or a man. And a girl; or a woman. They were almost as sharp and real as in one of my dreams. I could glimpse the outline of a forehead and nose, and when the man put his hand up to the girl's head his fingers were distinct for a moment before they blurred into a stroking movement he made over the girl's hair.

Their heads came together. Their mouths came together. His arms went round her, and their heads seemed to struggle one against the other.

I clutched the window frame, excited for no reason I could understand.

His hands kept moving, touching her

face and sliding downwards again. Once she stepped back, shaking her head so that the moonlight struck sparks from it; then he pulled her closer, and their heads merged into a strange shape that was silver, grey and black. And then they collapsed into the twilight between the wood stacks.

That night, when I had flopped back on to the bed, I went searching for other minds tuned in to what I had seen, or half seen: minds dreaming of other bodies, close, quivering with hunger, sometimes laughing and sometimes crying out. I followed couples through a confusing landscape, sharpening the picture when that landscape dissolved and there were just the two of them. Sometimes I got so close that they could feel me go past, or lean over them. With others, it was quite amusing to conjure up shapes in their minds, shapes they couldn't name which threatened to turn their warm, throbbing dreams into farce . . . or, if I was in mischievous mood, nightmares.

And then, as clearly as if it had been deliberately thrown at a couple to wake them up and drive them away, there appeared that stone again — like a heavy, twisted doughnut with that hole in the middle large enough for you to put your hand through.

It was there the next night, too, growing larger and clearer. And this time there was music in my head. Music all around, in a rhythm that made me want to dance. Who was playing this for me? I tried to grasp the strange lilt, the eccentric pulse of it all, and to follow the shifting cadences, mingling with something softer and too sentimental, yet with its own perverse enchantment. I was feeling things I hadn't felt before but which must have been waiting for me.

I must dream more deeply, explore further . . .

Somewhere there must be recognizable traces, which I could pick up, of those mysterious forces which so obsessed my father and which had driven two men to hunt me down. The source might be far away or, as my father was forever fearing, close at hand. Proximity, I was learning before I even learned the word itself, was not necessarily involved. A hundred miles in the solid outside world might be only a couple of paces, a second's change of direction, in dreamworld. You had to let your mind float, picked up by a breeze which carried you straight into a scene or chose to drift around it, past it, on towards some significant location, drawing you in like a magnet.

This was something my mother could have taught me, but she wanted to deny it and keep me away from it. She ought to have known better. She was denying herself and our family — our bloodline going back, I sensed by now, a long, long way.

There had to be a focus: something or someone I knew and could relate to.

Yes, here he was. I sensed him at once. Of course. Dominic Lynch again. And already he was half aware of me — or at any rate uneasily conscious of somebody or something sitting beside him. When he reached out to get a grip on somebody else's mind far away, my presence was causing him a slight drag. But he had no way yet of identifying me; and I would be careful not to let him have one.

For a long time now he had been taught in a different sort of establishment. They had put him through a tough training programme designed to ransack other men's minds. Not just drifting through them the way I enjoyed doing, but concentrating deep down, digging and planting. Working to distort, I began to realize, the technical applications of great powers of life and death — hideous death especially — in military calculations. Tied in with a régime halfway across the world, working along-side perverse elements closer to home.

Like a leech clinging to his probing mind, I went with Lynch into a tangle of experiments, which meant nothing coher-ent to either of us. There was a sudden surge of almost physical awareness as psychic emanations were aimed at dis-turbing various parts of the body, with special intensity against the bowels — a grisly echo of my own internal attack on that intruder.

And where did that phrase 'PsyOps' come floating in from? I caught glimpses of what looked like a school playground — no, a military centre — where

140

paranormal elements were being tested on the highest grade of martial arts trainees. Lynch was there, keeping to one side, waiting for orders to pick out one man and subject him to . . . well, to what?

Suddenly our two minds were engulfed by a screeching, scalding terror. A calculated mental plague, which had been stored up, waiting for the signal to trigger it off, was consuming the staff of the military centre, flowing outwards into the streets of the city, eating up the inhabitants. Literally eating them up. A pestilence formulated to eliminate enemy resistance by consuming their human flesh while leaving buildings intact was consuming its own people. I wanted to look away, or run away, but I could not pull myself free. Rushing towards me as if driven by a fiery wind, human bodies were convulsed in mad spasms of a grotesque dance, shedding their skin as it was dragged free by their burning clothes. Mouths opened and widened and went on gaping even wider as faces liquefied around them.

Then it all began to fade. I felt Lynch trying to keep a grip on it and force it to

141

obey his directions; but he was not up to it. It was slipping away through his grasp.

I was dragged with him, blundering between sleep and wakefulness, for a few fleeting moments into a small cell. A man shackled to a chair was trying to bend back, away from the pincers that were drawing closer and closer to his eyes.

'You will admit that you have been planning a terrorist campaign against the United States of America for the past five years?'

'No, I've never — '

A shaft of agony rasped like a serrated blade along and into my bone. I heard a smug, detached voice making some approving remark about 'enhanced interrogation techniques', and then . . . well, I can't say that I actually heard a long, shuddering scream, but somehow it seemed an appropriate accompaniment as I slid away and the world gradually steadied around me. I found that my breath was coming and going in violent gulps. Those minutes — or had it been hours? — of horror had sickened me. Yet at the same time — and to admit this was a horror in itself — there

142

had been a tang of awful pleasure tingling through my veins. It was like what I had achieved in destroying that deadly stalker, only much worse. And much more thrilling. Watching the flesh boiling, peeling away, unwrapping and crumpling up and sticking together like thin layers of plastic shredded from a colour magazine's plastic wrapper . . .

Lynch had given up and gone, leaving a question worrying enough in itself: was his the sort of task which had been meant for me, too, if I hadn't been taken and hidden away by my parents?

To cleanse my mind, I let myself float towards that stone which was coming to represent a steady, reliable point at the heart of all these other wanderings and whisperings.

And so I met Milada.

You get that, boy? Nestling there inside your mother, warm and comfortable, storing up all these words I'm committing to your receptive mind. You can now record the fact that this was where the two of us came together and made that heartfelt promise.

4

Some few days ahead I knew that my
father would be leaving and not coming
back. I had overheard him talking again
about us moving away. But where to?
Perhaps he was beginning to understand
that the men he was afraid of didn't just
operate in the physical, waking world but
could hunt one down in the depths of the
slumbering mind. Yet now, if he could
only have grasped that as well, he had no
need to be afraid of them. It could be left
to me. I was powerful enough to confuse
any intruders. They would have to find
stronger magic and stronger messengers.

Unhappily it wasn't something we could
discuss. To him I was an alien who had
brought all this upon him. He couldn't
accept the world which my mother knew
and which I knew even better.

So he wanted to get away and be done
with it.

My mother didn't want to believe it

when it happened. 'He must have had an accident. Or *they* . . . '

'No,' I said. 'Nobody's risked coming. Not for a long time. And he hasn't had an accident. He just couldn't take any more. He wasn't up to it.'

'You mustn't talk about your father like that.'

In spite of everything, she had always loved him. I'd had only a few glimmerings in my wanderings of what that sort of love was like, but with her I could tell it was real. And he had loved her — they wouldn't have been here together if he hadn't. But where did I come into it? Why had they bothered to have me if they were going to regret it in this way? So many questions; and such elusive answers.

I said: 'He's not coming back. You've got to accept that.'

She wanted to argue. But I knew that she was coming to regard me as her superior, the one whose knowledge was reaching far ahead of hers. Whatever we had in common, though, there was still that part of her that was an ordinary, susceptible woman.

Helplessly she said: 'The editor that he does all that work for, to keep us going. If they don't hear from him, they might send someone round looking for him. You must keep out of the way.'

'Maybe he told them he was going away.'

'He wouldn't tell them and not tell me.'

'Wouldn't he?'

She began to cry — silent crying, hunched in her chair, clutching her arms together.

In sleep that night, in spite of her having told me I mustn't do that sort of thing, I went looking for him.

He was nowhere to be found. Had he somehow been snared and been coaxed or forced into talking? But if that had happened, wouldn't the intensity of his fear — maybe physical pain — have come through to me? I opened my mind to whatever he could reveal, consciously or unconsciously. If he was looking for a job, maybe looking for another house, a flat, somewhere safer to hide, might I not come upon him in a roundabout way before he even guessed I was close at hand? There was no answering sensation, no response.

We were not in tune. It was as simple as that. My father was not one of us. *Us?* I was growing more and more aware of belonging to a family, a group, a privileged caste. In spite of her timidity, my mother and I belonged and my father didn't. He had drifted away, and was beyond reach now. I could not pick him up, in the way that one ceases to be able to pick up a fading radio signal.

In spite of that bond, my mother and I were finding it almost impossible to talk together now. I couldn't make up for my father's absence; and she seemed reluctant to reach out to me and share the knowledge, which was surely our common inheritance. Like those who had come stalking, she was scared of what I was capable of.

Alone I went wandering, listening, into places I had never seen. How could I visualize some of them so clearly when I had been pent up for so long and experienced so little? How could I hear and recognize sounds of a world in which

I had never walked — voices, the breeze through a coppice, the stabbing pee-wit, pee-wit or a plover, laughter of people I had never met? I was accumulating knowledge of places, some bright and immediate, some wispy and dissolving before I could get them in focus, all of them real in the night hours but unreachable when I was awake.

And now some force was directing me back, again and again, to the top of a low hill looking down on a stream that I had come to recognize. The more intently I stared at it, the more substantial it became.

Until one night the dream grass under my feet was as steady and tangible as the bed in my little room or the edge of the window frame to which I clung and still sometimes stole a peep out at the world. Everything had a clear edge, and I recognised the trees at the top of the slope and that bright curve of water below, embracing a short promontory with the dark brown shape rising from lush green grass. I went down confidently towards the stone, and reached it as a girl came along the bank of the stream.

I did not need to ask her name, and when she smiled at me it was obvious that she had been looking for me and was already content with what she knew about me. In dream, we instinctively knew more than anyone could ever have known in the realities of the waking world.

It was a joy to speak the name that had been there in my mind, waiting until it was ready to be spoken.

I said: 'Milada.'

Do you hear me, my son? My dear little boy, lying snug and warm in your mother's womb, assimilating everything I'm telling you so that it shall never be forgotten — this, dear lad, is how I first set eyes on your mother.

★   ★   ★

She was a slim little girl with a shy yet self-assured smile. Her bright chestnut hair was held back from her forehead by a turquoise band, matching the bronze sparkle in her eyes. She was wearing a light green summer frock that might almost have been woven from the landscape around her, and the glow in the skin of her arms and neck was an echo of the afternoon sunlight.

Afternoon? Was that what it was?

I wanted to touch those bare arms. Wanted to be close enough to breathe in the smell in the corner of her throat. Yet how did I know there would be such a scent and that I would be able to inhale it?

She rested her right hand on the top of the stone, I dared myself to walk closer, and put my right hand over hers. There was only the faintest tremor of a contact. We both moved slowly round the stone in a demure sort of dance, looking at each other all the time. The more we looked, the stronger the bond must become. I was begging her. No, not begging. Demanding on behalf of both of us. She must become real . . . had to become *touchable*.

I tried to get my fingers right round her hand and hold on to her, but everything dissolved and we were pulled apart as we woke up.

The memory lingered on into the

daylight hours. I found it hard to be jolted back into the reality of my mother's worries.

The gap left by my father was too huge for her to cope with. 'Somebody might have recognized him. Or he was . . . taken in for questioning.'

'Afraid he'll tell them where we are?'

'He wouldn't do that.' She hesitated, then blurted out: 'And you're not to lead them to him.'

'How on earth would I — '

'You're strong, but not strong enough to control yourself properly. Please, Patrick love, be careful. Listen. You must *listen*.'

'Who to? Sorry, Mother, but you can never tell me anything I don't already know.'

'Not me. There is the voice of the Wyrd, if you will only have the humility to listen.'

'Who on earth is the Wyrd?'

'You must be silent, and wait, and you will hear. The Wyrd is the One who was here before there were gods or a God, or priests of the gods . . . the One who had no beginning and will never end, but is always *becoming* . . . and forever watching and measuring.' Then her lips tightened and I could see she wished she hadn't spoken. There was just a last little reverent whisper: 'To whom we are all answerable.'

These words I'm dictating are not the words of a child. They are the summation today of everything I can clarify in my mind from those tantalizing days. Above all, from those nights.

Each day I waited impatiently for the next dreamworld meeting with Milada. Once or twice I tried to go to sleep in the daytime, but there was no way of forcing it. I had to wait until it all came about naturally. There were too many dismal moments or hours when there was no sign of Milada. Had she lost interest — or been forbidden to meet me?

Instead of the joy of meeting her again, I was suddenly shaken by quite another sort of encounter. It was a summons for which I had perhaps been half expecting, a recall to unfinished business.

★   ★   ★

Once more I was with Dominic Lynch. At first he was unaware of my presence at his shoulder. On the borders of sleep, he was waiting to sink fully under, not sure he would be able to cope with what was asked of him. I kept very still, not wanting to jolt him back into wakefulness, waiting to slide unobtrusively in beside him.

We were in a cramped little room with a window looking down into that cell with whitewashed walls which I had glimpsed before, its only furniture a plain narrow bed or table with three sets of straps dangling loose. As we watched, it was bleary at first — because Dominic was still not fully asleep and was seeing things in that same unfocussed way. The vague outline of a man was brought in on a trolley, and presumably there were two real men there to lift him off it and on to the table, but their bodies and faces were transparent and faded away once their skeletal hands had finished fastening the straps to hold the prone figure down.

Another man came closer to the table

and looked questioningly up — directly at Dominic and myself, it seemed.

'All right, Slee.' The voice, a real voice from a world awake, came from behind us. 'Put him out.'

Slee, whoever he might be, leaned over the prone figure and carefully directed a long needle into his left arm. For a few seconds the man came to life, fighting against the straps, struggling to push upwards, and then sighed. It was barely a sound at all, but I was acutely conscious of that long, eerie sigh.

'OK, he's out.' This was louder and more ordinary.

At the same time I felt Dominic sinking very slowly, and as he did so the outlines of the cramped space below sharpened, and the blur of a face became clearly that of a dark-skinned man with a ragged swirl of darker beard.

'Right, then,' said that voice behind us. 'Get to work, Lynch.'

Like a leech clinging to his probing mind, I went with Dominic into the drugged world of that unconscious creature, reaching in, ready to play on his fears and create new ones for him.

'You realize things will be better for you if you speak before the real pressure is applied? Like this, for instance . . . '

The answering groans and sobs were meaningless; but richly gratifying.

We had to go deeper. Probe into the depths where it would hurt more, frighten most. For this mental torture to work and leave the subject vulnerable to the following physical torture planned for him, it was essential to plant something too foul for the conscious mind to accept.

Reaching to inflict a more intense pain, all at once I found myself hearing music. It came flooding over me — not so much an accompaniment as an essential part of the agony. Harsh, barbaric music, full of brassy discords, its remorseless rhythm driving harder and harder, notes too high to be audible screeching in my ears and jarring down my spine until I could have wept with the torment of it but at the same time found myself shuddering with a wild joy. I could feel right through myself the victim's sufferings, and drowned myself ecstatically in them.

But then they began ebbing away. I sensed Dominic was beginning to feel sick, like a child sickened by a scary fairy tale he had enjoyed at first but now didn't want to continue. He tried moving his head away, but in dream it was still locked to the calculated nightmare. I was carrying him along with me, forcing him to share what was there, dominating the whole picture, which glowed before his eyes and through his eyes into his mind. I was making it as terrible for him as it was for the man on that table. I was in charge. I was brushing him aside, intent only on destroying that pathetic wretch strapped down there at my mercy. Mercy?

Somebody was muttering a question behind me. It was the voice of somebody wide awake, but knowledgeable enough to be impatient with what they were trying to guess was happening in that shared trance of Dominic and his victim — or not happening quite the way it had been planned. Somewhere they were suspecting something.

I could have told them that Dominic was lacking the real guts for the job.

Hadn't they taught him *anything* at that school?

The unsteadiness of his squeamish mind was cluttering up my own. In a rage I used all the strength I could muster, picturing hot skewers twisting their way into the prisoner's eyes, and felt an answering shriek of utter despair from below. Then Dominic was trying to wake up, and I was losing the picture he had created for me. Dream and reality merged and faded.

'Christ, the bastard's dead.' An accusing voice outside my head.

'The clumsy sod's gone too far. That wasn't the brief.'

One of them was more alert than the others. On the last fringes of that dream I heard the frustration in a daytime voice. 'That wasn't Lynch. It's *him*. That one who got away.'

'Get a hold on him. Don't let him go this time.'

But I shook them off and ran away into wakefulness.

★   ★   ★

157

If I had wanted a reward for my accomplishment, I got it. Lying in bed, I relaxed for half an hour or so, and then closed my eyes and let myself float towards that stone, the one reliable, steady point at the heart of all these wanderings and whisperings. And she was there, waiting, quite smartly dressed this time as if she was going to a party. Yet what did I know about parties? I couldn't imagine going to one with her, or indeed going to any such thing on my own. Yet I felt stupidly jealous. I forced myself to concentrate and care only that she was here by the water's edge, and that both she and the stone were growing more and more real.

She said: 'My father, he tells me there is nothing of this kind in the country we come from.'

'Another country?'

She told me its name, but it meant nothing. Just a scattering of odd sounds strung together.

'He thinks to bring me here,' she said, 'to get away.'

'Away from what?' I thought of being

taken away from that school; and she caught on to my thought and smiled sympathetically but only half understanding.

I was determined everything should be clearer. As if to obey me, the sun came out and the world grew brighter and sharp-edged, and Milada was real and knew it, too. Briefly I was frightened that I had lost her. The little girl was no longer there. Instead, there was the answer to questions I had not so far had the confidence to pose. She was the shape of a woman, gazing at me directly and without concealment.

As I drew closer she went down on her knees in the grass and put her hand through the hole in the handfasting stone, a little girl playing a game, yet as determined and as sure of herself as the grown woman I was determined must last on beyond this dream and into reality. Laughing, she waved her fingers at me, beckoning me closer.

I, too, went down on my knees. On the other side of the stone, I put out my fingers to interlace with hers.

She went on looking at me, her chin on the stone, sweet and desirable . . . and puzzled. 'This, please, I do not know what comes next.'

I tightened my grip on her fingers. 'We shall be handfasted.'

'Please?'

I said: 'Swear that for one year from this day you will be faithful to me.'

'Only a year?'

'Swear it.'

'I swear. And after that,' she said gently, 'forever.' She looked so deep into my eyes that I was afraid of what she might find. 'And you?' she said.

'I will be faithful to you. Until the year is up. And then we decide whether to continue, or whether to part. Without reproach.'

Our hands were warm and real. No longer a wraith of a handclasp.

'Handfast.' She tried the word out and to her, I saw, it was music. 'So we are handfasted until either of us wishes that it should be renounced. A year, yes . . . or surely much, much longer?'

Over her sweet-smelling shoulder I

thought I saw movement among the trees. A shape like a leafless, diseased branch cast a malignant shadow on the undergrowth beneath: no more than a wraith, but one darkening and threatening to put on substance. Dominic Lynch, seeking revenge for the insults that had been heaped on him after I had left? Becoming dangerously aware of Milada, so real and vibrant, waiting? I forced myself not to alarm her. She went on looking lovingly at me, clinging to my hand, not turning to look over her shoulder. But then, as we tried to kiss, she melted away and I was awake again, in a world that was coming to mean nothing without her.

You still listening, boy? Nestling there inside your mother, warm and comfortable, grateful that she and I were destined to come together and create you?

The promise was so exquisite at the time. Yet was condemned to be so foully broken.

5

There came a morning when my mother made a decision. She said nothing about it to me, but I suspected she might have had a letter, and I wondered what she had in mind for us. In the night hours I risked trying to enter her dreams, but she kept them closed against me. There was no way in, she was able to resist me where few others would have been capable of it. Surely, since we shared that same aptitude, we ought to have been able to converse on the same level in the same language — or without the need for language. But love for an outsider had contaminated her. She would not share with me.

If she wouldn't yield, there was nothing for it but to ask her outright.

'What are you thinking of doing?'

'There's nothing to worry about, my sweet. It'll all be all right.'

She bustled away from the kitchen and made a big fuss about cleaning the bathroom. Whenever she was somewhere else and I was thinking about her, I always visualized her in one particular way. She would be standing with her head turned to one side so that her nose seemed rather big, and her lips were slightly parted and she looked puzzled. It was a faraway sort of puzzlement, as if she was provoked by something she could never hope to grasp. And then she would close her mouth very firmly, snapping it shut on a haphazard decision.

This day she had indeed made one. Half an hour later she was back with her hat and coat on. I wanted to grab her and make her take them off. She was surely not going out looking for my father? She couldn't just go out searching at random. Or had there indeed been a letter, risking asking her to meet him somewhere?

She said: 'I'm going out to look for a job.'

'But — '

'We've got to have some money.' She was brisk and matter-of-fact about it. 'And while I'm out, I might see about finding us somewhere else to live.'

Because somewhere my father might at this very moment be answering questions? She might not want to believe that. But still she would feel safer if we had moved on.

The two of them had hoped that before. She insisted on wheeling me into my own room. 'Now you must promise me to stay here until I get back. Don't go into the sitting room, anywhere near the window. Don't go in there at all, right?'

'Right,' I said. 'All right.'

She looked at me doubtfully, and spoke more slowly and clearly. 'If anyone comes to the front door, pay no attention. I'm not expecting any deliveries or anything. There's nothing to be afraid of. The door'll be locked, and nobody can get in.'

'Right,' I said again. 'Yes, all right.'

'You'll be perfectly safe if you do as I say.'

'Yes,' I said.

She kissed me and went out. I felt the thud of the front door closing. I was on my own. I felt less at ease than I usually did when I was alone.

Was she going to come back?

I longed for the safety and sureties of dream; but I was too wide-awake to be capable of steering myself into my special, dependable world.

She had been gone about twenty minutes, perhaps longer, when I ventured out of my room and propelled myself along the corridor. The curtains were drawn back, so that even from the door into the sitting room I felt exposed. It was a bright day. Light gleamed in a bowl on the window-ledge, and the houses across the street appeared very close. I stood half in, half out of the room. When somebody walked along the far side of the street I dodged back. This was daylight, unreliable. I felt exposed.

I admit that I must have left my room as a gesture of defiance. My room was the only safe place. It was my home, and I could never leave it. Never, that is, until I went out hand in hand with Milada. I went back where I belonged, and turned on my radio. The music this morning had a welcome sharp taste to it. I felt it tart on my tongue as well as in my ears. When the first piece had finished, the announcer said something I couldn't understand about Dallapiccola and the duodecaphonic influence of Webern, whose Five Movements for String Quartet would follow. I was not so much listening as inhaling it, letting it seep inwards.

I sprawled on my bed as more notes bit through my skin in spasmodic stabs, twisting their way towards something I knew must be a fulfilment. The effect managed to be both stimulating and hypnotic. I closed my eyes, willing myself not to be here.

Why was there a dense, threatening blackness framing the idyllic setting I had been looking for? The whole familiar scene was being squeezed into such a small space that to reach the water's edge I found myself stepping over that black rim as if over a doorstep.

And then I was back where I wanted to be, and Milada was approaching along the bank.

When I reached my hand out to hers once more, the mere touch of our fingers sent a resonance like pungent music through our bodies.

'It's not enough,' I said. I was impatient for us to meet in the flesh, on solid ground, in daylight.

'I think this must be our reality for now, my love.' The words came out gently, reluctantly, exploring an idea she couldn't be sure of. I yearned for her, yet at the same time I was angry and impatient. I couldn't be doing with her not being as impatient as myself. 'We must keep thinking ourselves deeply into togetherness,' she murmured, 'and then it will all happen, it must happen.'

I think I was about to seize her brutally by the shoulders and shake her and insist that everything had to happen now, right here and now, when two heavy thuds seemed to come from the heart of the stone, and she vanished as if tossed away by the impact.

I was jolted awake.

★   ★   ★

There came another double knock at the front door. I swung my legs over the edge of the bed, sitting absolutely still. If nobody in here answered, then whoever it

167

was might go away.

It came yet again, much louder this time. Had I somehow given myself away? They could possibly have picked up my dream intensities and been led here at last. Led here, even, by Dominic Lynch, forever resentful and bent on my humiliation.

I swung myself from the bed into my wheelchair, at the same time willing the intruders to go away. But I had no powers in this daylight world; I could not control things as I did when sleep had embraced those folk who mattered.

When the noise began again, it came from the back of the house. The kitchen door was not as heavy as the front door, and began creaking as the pounding on it turned into a heavier assault.

I must get out of the house before they smashed their way into it.

It was an idea almost as terrifying as the thought of those men doing whatever they were going to do to me. Out of the house . . . on my own.

And when my mother came back . . . what would she be faced with?

I looked up at the skylight.

If I could get out on to the roof and stay up there very quiet, they wouldn't see me. They would find the house empty and would assume I'd gone out somewhere with my parents. They weren't to know, after all, that we never did go out like that, all three of us.

The skylight seemed so close, a simple way out. A crazy notion, all right. But I was in a panic.

I dragged my way up as usual, but much faster and riskier, and got the window open. The sun was dazzling. I felt myself slipping, and groped with my good foot; but there was nothing immediately below it. I tried desperately to stiffen my arms. Just when I thought I would have to let myself go and fall back on the bed, I managed to wedge my right elbow across the window frame. It gave me enough breathing space to give another push with my left arm.

I swung myself over the frame. Most of my weight was outside now. My finger-nails scrabbled over the smooth tiles. I hauled myself right out, letting my legs slide gently down the slope while I kept a grip on the frame.

When I let myself look around, I felt dizzy. It wasn't the height: it was the extent of space, all around me and above me. The sky was a great sweep of smoky blue, with one splash of cloud shot through with a streak of sunlight. I felt I was going to fall upwards into it. Looking up or down, I was sure I was going to fall.

I put my palms down flat on the roof, keeping me where I was. The full danger of it hit me now.

Even if the men who were after me didn't look out on to the roof, they might stay in the house for ages. They might wait there on the alert until my mother came back.

It was that which drove me on. I had to get down to the yard so that I could hide somewhere — behind that woodpile, maybe — and keep a lookout for my mother coming back. I must warn her not to go into the house.

I began to edge along the roof. Once I had moved away from the window, I had to go slowly. There was nothing to hold on to. I must just shuffle and wriggle along, pausing and trying to stop my gasps of breath getting too loud.

What I would do when I got to the end, I had no idea.

There was quite a way to go. It appeared that the house we lived in was the end of a row of terraces. I could drop to the street, which ran along the front of the houses but then where would I go? In any case it was risky. Those men down below might have come out and started looking here, there, up and along.

Slowly I eased myself down towards the gutter. Something kept tugging at me — an urge to let go, to let myself slide right off and out into space. And the sky made me dizzier.

It was the abrupt flicker of something in the corner of my eye that jabbed me into motion. I saw the head of a man emerging from our skylight, heard him shout, and at once let myself go over the edge of the roof. My fingers clawed instinctively for the gutter, and missed. My knuckles rasped down the rough brick of the wall. I fell, awkwardly. Then I hit the ground.

There was an explosion of pain through my left leg, worse than anything I'd ever suffered before. The flagstones of the yard seemed to buckle and sway like the waves of the sea in front of my eyes. I wanted to give up. Just lie back and let the worst happen. Let myself drown in unconsciousness. But I realized that I was only a couple of yards from the back gate. In a haze of agony I heaved myself over that last gap and groped upwards for the latch. It was very loose — probably why those trespassing shapes I had seen had found it so easy to get in.

I could hear nothing apart from the gulping echo of my own breathing inside my head, but soon there would surely be more shouts as the men called to one another, working out the way I had gone.

In a trance I was trying to will myself into getting up and running, as I could have done in dream. But this was the outside world. I had not been out in the open for years, and everything was too high and too wide. The street ran away at all angles; topsy-turvy buildings bent over me, threatening to crumble on top of me, or else leaned backwards in a fantastic stagger.

'Come on,' I was howling to myself. 'Come on, get up — you've *got* to.'

There was the sound of someone blundering across the yard behind me. Something swung round the corner of the street ahead of me — a shining silvery car. I had seen such things through the school railings, read about them at home and seen them racing at me from a television screen, but never seen one as large and frightening as this.

It swept in beside me and jolted to a stop. The back door opened. A hand reached out, a man was stooping towards me.

'Come on, Patrick. Just in time.'

I was dragging myself absurdly back along the pavement.

'Come on, old lad. We're friends.'

'No,' I was shouting. 'No, leave me alone.'

In sleep, in dream, I could have beaten them, driven them off. But here in daylight I was powerless.

A man was out of the car. He got a grip

on me, and heaved me bodily through the open rear door. My leg banged against the door itself, and then I had been dragged right in, falling into a heap, my cheek against something scrubby on the floor. The door slammed, the floor trembled under me. Someone was trying to lift me into a sitting position, pushed against the back of the seat. Everything was swaying to and fro. A flicker of houses and windows spun dizzily away on either side.

'Let me out.'

They had found me. They were taking me away.

'It's all right.' The man in the seat beside me put an arm round my shoulders, but I pulled away. 'It's all right,' he went on in a voice I couldn't trust. 'We've found you in time. You're safe now. Safe from those others.'

The world went on lurching to and fro. The continual movements of the car were terrifying. I wanted to shout out, but who would pay any attention? Then the ragged blur of houses drifted away to either side and began to give way to a line of low, dark green hills and glimpses of bright blue sky.

'Dr. Lanner, we got him.'

'Nice work.' It was a tinny voice, the sort of sound I would get off the radio when it had somehow shifted off station. 'High time, too.'

'He's not in good shape, I'm afraid.'

'We've got him. That's what counts.'

Then blackness descended. I went down with it, and for a long time there was a darkness without any dreams.

Part Three

RESONANCES

1

First there was the rumble of the stairlift making its slow way down from the tower, then the click of straps being undone, and the arm of a wheelchair being snapped back into place. The tyres squeaked as the chair was spun at an angle to come smoothly through the doorway.

Patrick Robson at seventeen was a long way on from the boy Hugo Lanner's hired paramedics had plucked from the street outside his house. He was tall, slim rather than skinny, with a shock of auburn hair that looked startlingly alive above those impassive blue eyes. Wheeling himself into the sunshine filled room, he moved slowly, as if just waking up.

He could have looked resentful, confined to that chair — 'Since that second fall finished off his leg for good,' as Hugo had once put it to Ruth without ever explaining any first fall. Yet he seemed

179

cool and detached. If he had been a completely free agent, would he still be here as Hugo's protégé . . . or prisoner?

He said: 'All right, how far have you got, playing with ideas for this Valence nonsense? Needs two or three spring-boards, right? One top level, two in the distribution chain. There's no way I can influence the entire buying public. Have to choose individual targets.'

'We've already established that at the meeting,' said Hugo. 'In this case, we could start with — '

'With the manager of a major store,' said Patrick. His voice had become an incantatory drone. 'There's one within my reach. I can encourage him to persuade his staff to give prominence to the new Valence product. At the same time I suggest the usual media advertising should incorporate a sincere young woman. Not one of the over-used actresses or models. For the television campaign and in the fashion magazines choose a physically attractive unknown, and let me secretly teach her to be sincere.'

'To be sincere?' said Ruth. 'Without knowing it?'

'But of course. Smooth mannerisms are easily seen through. I'd inculcate an image to convince everybody looking at her that in recommending a product she *must* be telling the truth.' There was no emotion in his voice as he stated what to him needed no discussion. 'And it occurs to me that we might consider weakening the opposition right from the start.'

'The opposition?' Ruth thought that here at least they must be talking the same language. 'Of course we're aware that the main problem would be a conflicting campaign by Valence's main rival — part of their even bigger aim of taking them over. If we can outguess them — '

'I think that for a start I should contact the managing director of Lauriston Cosmetics and persuade him to press ahead with a crude marketing campaign which falls flat alongside ours. By the time his reps have realized this, it'll be too late. Or perhaps find a way of getting them to cook their own books without getting even a glimmering of where they've gone wrong. And then,' Patrick went on with the nearest approach to enthusiasm Ruth had yet heard from him, 'I'll concentrate on the producer of the current television fashion programme. Just a few hints into her sleeping subconscious . . . a touch so subtle she won't even realize what she's saying, but feels utterly convinced by it.'

Ruth had a dizzying vision of Patrick with tentacles like those of a computer hacker probing not into laptops and mobiles but directly into minds, which mistakenly thought themselves in control of all their own desires.

Hugo was about to say something when there was a rap on the door.

Mrs. Storey had arrived with tea.

★ ★ ★

Elaine Storey had been nurse to the family before its last member married Hugo Lanner, brought him home with her; and died. Hugo had persuaded Ruth and Matthew that she should stay on the payroll when ownership of Burntrigg came into the hands of the Copsholm company: they needed someone with the right qualifications to keep Patrick 'in working order', as he put it. Of her own accord Mrs. Storey had taken on other household tasks; but if ever she had been referred to or even hinted at as a housemaid or part-time cook, she would almost certainly have walked out without a further word.

She had a pinched little mouth, which expressed quiet disapproval even though she never uttered a presumptuous word. Her dress was always dark grey, always trim and tight and always impeccably clean. She was in her late thirties, but her severely brushed near-flaxen hair made her look older. There was never any reference to a Mr. Storey, and she wore no wedding ring. She seemed half in awe of Patrick, half wryly humorous about him, as if caring for an amusing pet while at the same time keeping a wary eye open in case it snapped at her.

It had become her custom, whenever her present employers were 'in conference', as she sceptically described it, to serve tea at what she estimated to be the halfway mark, even though not summoned to do so. Now she moved to set the tea tray down on Hugo's desk, silently urging him to push his papers to one side.

Then she turned her attention to Patrick.

'Only just spotted the stairlift was down. Thought you were still up there with your music.'

Your music . . . It might have been a minor ailment they had all learnt to tolerate; or an eccentricity beyond everyday discussion. And it implied that she would now have to go and fetch another cup and saucer.

'I don't particularly want anything, thanks.'

'It's no trouble. No trouble at all.'

They had to wait for her to go back downstairs and return with another cup and saucer and another two of her chocolate buns.

When she had finally left the room, Patrick appeared to have gone into a trance for some minutes, then finished a bun, wiped his lips delicately with a napkin.

'And then there's the possibility of approaching them sideways on. Testing the ground via search engines on the web. Pick the most influential ones — people with clout on selected blogs.'

'Trying to find the important ones would take up an awful lot of time,' protested Hugo. 'You'd find it very wearing.'

'I can cope,' said Patrick complacently. 'People who rely so much on these things have very loosely coordinated minds. Very easy to whisper in their ears. Tell them what they're subconsciously ready to hear. So that they believe they've come up with a whole wonderful idea all by themselves. And the opposition . . . ' He was staring into the distance, far beyond the stone walls of this room. 'Try to disturb *their* sleep. Distract them.'

'Isn't that a bit — '

'Leave it to me.' Patrick's fingers tightened around the wheels of his chair and spun it slowly towards the door. 'Let me wander. And,' he said, 'stay out of my way.'

There was almost an implication that

he would be quite prepared to run them down if they obstructed him.

* * *

When he had gone, Ruth said: 'Doesn't he ever demand a motorized chair? And surely some sort of prosthesis could have been fitted by now.'

'Not without the risk of drawing attention to his whereabouts. Word would have got back — '

'All the same, I'd have thought that by now, at his age, he'd have been clamouring for means of a bit more freedom. Freedom of movement, I mean.'

'Nights out on the town? No, definitely not. We had difficulty enough getting our hands on him. We can't risk them grabbing him back.'

'But look at him. Don't you feel some responsibility for . . . well, I mean, he's a normal, healthy lad. Must have . . . well, the usual appetites. He must want to meet girls in the normal way. Go out for an evening, that sort of thing.'

'He's quite content to stay in for the

evening,' said Hugo severely. 'And the night. With his dreams.'

'Is that the best he can hope for?'

'Sooner or later he may find his true opposite number. The results could be awe-inspiring. '

'Sounds like trying to find the mate for a giant panda in a zoo.' She stared a challenge at him. 'You said something about him being grabbed back by . . . whoever had him before. Meaning he's not quite so unique? You hinted there could be others?'

'Oh, yes. There are others. Members of that long bloodline, going a long way back. The Gifted Ones. That's what that school of his was about.'

'And there might be a chance their minds might all try, one day, to meet up? Get together as members of the family?'

'Yes, I do wonder about that. Whether it would be an interesting development — or a terrifying one.'

Ruth wondered whether in some ways Hugo's scientific interests might not be too abstract. He was not unduly con-cerned whether an experiment — with a

human situation or a human heart
— worked out to a happy ending or a
tragedy.

Above them the music began again.
This time there was something barbaric
in it. 'Let me wander,' Patrick had said.
Seeking a challenge, perhaps. And what
might the response to that be?

In the old days there had been many
attempts to set fire to the lower floor of
the tower and smoke the defenders out.
Ruth wondered uneasily if the modern
building was strong enough to withstand
a modern assault — perhaps a sly,
undermining one.

2

Jeremy Deverell had been head buyer for the Magasin Modes Group for five years, after ten years of working his way up and elbowing rivals out of the way. It had all been done with a smile as smooth as the women's faces in the Group's advertising photographs, just as his clothes had always had to be a suitably suave accompaniment to those which their favoured clients tended to wear. He enjoyed most days of his working life, but this one promised to be very special.

The Group was opening a brand-new store. A large proportion of its sales came from concessions within large department stores. In the past five years, during which Jeremy could boast that he had been involved with crucial decisions on marketing, three self-contained ventures had been set up. One, in Edinburgh, had failed to show a profit. The other two, in York and in the Group's Norwich headquarters, were progressing healthily. And now there was to be this much more speculative outlet: a smart white building on the edge of the Gretna Outlet complex, tempting traffic in from the motorway thundering across the Border between England and Scotland.

Jeremy disliked the sound of bagpipes, but it was inevitable that on the grand opening day two pipers should be positioned near the entrance. He waited outside, with two of his female staff, smart in their company uniform of crisp white jacket and skirt, its austerity relieved by a pale mauve collar. The big boss back in Norwich had decreed long ago that staff should never look too wiltingly feminine, in case they made lady customers jealous. Better to have a touch of the authoritarian, capable of telling the customer what was good for her.

The two were carrying bouquets ready to present to the visiting dignitaries whose cars were circling the Outlet complex and coming to rest as the pipers set off furiously on what Jeremy supposed might be a triumphal victory march. He was glad to escort the visitors into the air-conditioned interior and to give the nod for the main doors to be closed again, shutting out the skirling. Here inside, the cool pastel shades of the raked ceiling and the display counters were echoed in piped music of a different kind which to Jeremy was agreeably innocuous.

There came the even more musical sound of champagne corks popping. Bouquets which had been handed over were smoothly handed on further to a retinue of hired flunkeys. Speeches were short and pleasantly meaningless. After a mere twenty minutes the doors were reopened to admit the public.

Sleek young reps and some thin young women began circulating, handing out samples and leaflets. Jeremy set about re-checking each counter and display. One saw everything more intensely now that the place was open. He listened amiably to sales talk from an eager young rep and shrugged him off with a skill acquired on many a shop floor over many years.

It was not until the middle of the afternoon that the first rush had calmed down, and clusters of shoppers were settling into the coffee bar and deciding where to go next, or whether to go home. A chance now for him to approach Karen with the perfectly good excuse of checking on progress.

'Good brisk opening, wouldn't you say, Mrs. Larsen?'

'Going very well, Mr. Deverell.'

'Another couple of hours, and we can all relax, eh?'

Karen Larsen was a tall divorcée who gave a first impression of being the typical ice-cold blonde, belied with the warmth of her smile, her habit of leaning confidingly a few inches towards one, and the slight lisp when she spoke. Traces of her Danish upbringing still lingered. Her flawless face had been so well pampered that it would take the treatments of another ten years to tauten into wrinkles. Jeremy remembered the challenge that the ice-maiden appearance had seemed to offer when they first met; and how tantalizing it had been to wait for the thaw, the feeling of her being kept in storage for him, waiting to be defrosted.

Now that private little smile of hers acknowledged what he was suggesting, but all she said coolly was: 'Quite a day. We've had nearly as many would-be sellers as we've had buyers. An eager beaver from Lauriston, and hard on his heels a fussy little female from Valence — '

'Oh, Valence. Yes, they've been after me as well with some new cream of theirs. Miracle workers, all of them, these skin rejuvenating lotions, toners — '

'Reversing sun and wind damage and rebinding seriously dehydrated skin,' she took him up.

'You sound just like that Zoë something-or-other. Not to mention the busy-busy prodding one gets from that pushy little boss of hers.'

He did not mention that he had briefly shared some of Zoë's favours a week ago, though without following up any of her business suggestions.

'But don't knock it,' said Karen. 'It's our livelihood!'

He leaned towards her. 'As a matter of

193

interest, what's that *you're* wearing?'

'Like it?'

'I prefer it when you're wearing nothing.'

She glanced down at her left wrist. 'Synchronize watches?'

★ ★ ★

They met at a hotel on the fringe of the Lake District, an hour's drive south of the Border. Karen had changed into a flamboyant puce dress that clung to her breasts, leaving her bare shoulders creamy under the subdued lighting in the restaurant. It had been a busy day, but a rewarding one. The buzz of the opening was still with them, and neither of them was tired. Which didn't mean they were in no hurry to get to bed.

As they finished the meal, Karen looked over her left shoulder, up at the wall.

'Isn't there something odd about that music?'

He had not been aware of any of the usual piped music, but now he heard

194

something and, without knowing why, agreed it was odd. There was something hypnotic in its repetitive phrases, as if someone was humming without knowing quite how to round off the phrases ... drawing one in, with a tinge of mockery, challenging the listener to finish the cadence.

Jeremy raised a finger to summon the head waiter.

'What exactly is that muzak you're playing?'

The man frowned. 'We don't have muzak here, sir.'

'Well whatever you call it. The music. It's so peculiar. We've been trying to guess what it is.'

The man was looking at them uneasily. 'There's no music here, sir. None at all. It's our policy never to annoy guests with that sort of thing.' He summoned up a lofty smile. 'No canned food, no canned music.'

When he had gone away they both sat very still, listening. It became even stranger. There were no obvious speakers in the corners of the ceiling and not what you could really call a sound. Yet they looked at each other and nodded, and agreed: a voice was singing its way into their heads, mocking but luring them on.

They finished the meal and did not wait for coffee.

In bed, he let his hands wander over her in slow appreciation, flattered by the pounding of her heart and the growing urgency of her own hands and her mouth. The prelude to an age-old ritual.

Afterwards, they both drifted away into exhausted sleep.

The last thing of which he was conscious was the smell of her shoulder. Puzzling. Earlier there had been the perfume of which she was so fond and which he would always associate with her. Yet now there was something on her skin which he only half recognized, which for some reason he knew he had been brushing aside somewhere, somehow.

Crazily it followed him into dreams. When had he ever before been conscious of scents in dreams? Some people said you couldn't dream in colour, but he knew that was ridiculous. He was always conscious of colours around him, and tonight he was in an unusually beautiful woodland, with a young woman beside him — not Karen, not his wife, not any of the girls he had known so far, but one he had always yearned to meet — and the sun sprinkled fascinating shadows through the trees, and there was this glorious, mesmerizing smell.

It was still there when he woke up in the morning, but blew away as Karen groped drowsily for him. Half asleep, they made love again, and then she went off into the bathroom. He heard her muttering something to herself, and when she came out she sat on the edge of the bed, leaning toward him, and said: 'Funny, but my skin toner . . . I don't smell right, do I?'

He sniffed. 'No. But it's the usual stuff, isn't it?'

'Only it's gone off somehow.'

'Skin creams shouldn't go off. Not the expensive ones, anyway.' This was his speciality, goodness knows. 'Not unless there's a belated skin reaction. People's metabolism does change, I suppose.'

'Just a minute. I don't really fancy it, but . . . '

She went into the bathroom again. When she came back and leaned over him again, he said: 'My God, that's a lot more like.'

'I can't believe it. I wouldn't have thought — '

'Come here.' He breathed her in, reached out his hands for her.

At breakfast they ate in silence for quite a time. Not quite silence, though. There was that background music again; but this morning it was strangely soothing: in some way, ridiculously, approving. He was not going to risk raising the subject with the waiter, though it was a different young man at this time of day. But every now and then he was aware of Karen glancing at him as if to broach a subject and then deciding not to risk it. He had gone through situations like this before, when a girl was trying to summon up the courage to come out with some cliché about it being better for them not to see each other again; though usually he had been the one to decide when it was time to call it a day. He was by no means ready for it to happen with Karen yet.

He broke the silence. 'Look. I've been thinking. Sounds crazy, but maybe we were wrong about that Valence product. Don't know why it's been pestering me, but — '

'That's what I've been using,' she said. 'That's what I changed to this morning. I had that sample pot, and I . . . well, somehow I just *felt* . . . '

'I'm supposed to be in York for lunch, but I think they'll have to wait. I suggest I come back to the Gateway with you and we go through that order book and do a bit of a rethink.'

They both laughed, the rueful laughter of two business associates who had reluctantly come to an agreement, which ought to have been reached long ago.

The staff found themselves clearing space for new displays that Mr. Deverell had managed at remarkably short notice to arrange with Valence Enterprises. Jeremy enjoyed moments like these, when a major reorganization could be achieved by lunchtime.

As he left the main showroom, Karen said: 'You'll be calling in from time to time, to check on turnover?'

'All sorts of turnover,' he said. 'But of course.'

He was still in a mood to stir things up by the time he reached York. Yes, it was true they had decided not to stock Valence products. But there had been a change of policy. It wasn't a matter for discussion. Jeremy still enjoyed the shiver of apprehension that could be made to run along the floor at his appearance. Today he set the mood by telling off a salesgirl who had shown up for work in a grey trouser suit with a floral cravat, which was quite the wrong image. Give them no warning what to expect. Keep them on their toes.

Or one of them, anyway, on her back.

He was running far too late to get home that night. Bryony was quite ready to accept his excuses: in business these things happened, and it would be silly for an intelligent wife to ask questions. Life was too cosy to be disrupted. And Miriam was always glad to see him, even at such rare intervals and usually unannounced. A widow in her forties, she was an essential member of the Magasin Modes branch, mingling the suave sales techniques taught to all staff with a Yorkshire bluffness for customers of a certain age from the surrounding country-side and small towns.

She would sometimes put on a deliber-ately exaggerated accent with Jeremy when they were in bed. 'Eeh, Mr. Deverell' — she always called him Mr. Deverell with a throaty chuckle — 'that were reet grand. Get your breath back, and let's do it again, mm?'

The dreams were almost the same, filled with light and colour, and the smell he had now had hours of practice in identifying as the new Valence product. And this time there was that music — twisted a bit, provocative, as if someone was sup-plying him with uninvited tape music of a sort he wouldn't have invited — in the dream itself. Music to accompany a performance of some kind, as if he and Miriam were two glove puppets, one on each hand of a puppet master.

Who was thinking that, somewhere out of sight, laughing at them as his ghostly fingers manipulated them?

Ridiculous.

When they woke in the early morning light, Miriam said grumpily: 'I'm smelling that new stuff on me all the time, even though I haven't touched it.'

'It's nice, isn't it?'

'Not so sure it's *me*. I think most of our customers nowadays go much more for something with a touch of — '

'They'll go for this.' Even only half awake, he was still capable of giving decisive orders.

If only there wasn't that weird echo in the background, that self-satisfied laugh and an indulgent pat on the back that he felt even though nothing could possibly have touched him.

The music went on inside his head for a while as he left for home early in the morning.

Bryony was lying elegantly on the chaise-longue in an emerald crepe evening dress, although it was only mid-afternoon. It had to be admitted that even after eight years of marriage she could still maintain, even for her husband, the soignée appearance of her days in the model agency from which he had plucked her. She had also managed to put behind her the fact that her real name was Madge.

He stooped over her for the routine kiss.

She sniffed. 'You've got yourself a pretty weird aftershave. Not what I'd call masculine.'

'Damn it, I must have spilt one of our latest samples when I was packing my bag.'

'Samples of what?'

'I think you may change your mind when you've really tried it. We all took against it at first, but it's grown on us.'

Something else she had comfortably put behind her was any curiosity about who 'we' might be. She simply nodded and yawned, waiting for him to go and pour them a drink.

* * *

'Too easy,' said Patrick Robson. 'Hardly worth the effort.'

Hugo Lanner was always very wary

about criticizing his charge's vagaries too bluntly. The young man was an asset to be treated delicately and not damaged by too impatient an approach.

At this moment he looked not so much defiant as utterly uninterested in what was going on around him. He had been reluctant to turn off his music — a Bach partita, Hugo recognized, which usually meant he was in a relaxed mood, though the relaxation disappeared when he was interrupted.

'No! No, we can't — not there, you can't expect me to leave it on an uncompleted cadence like that!'

Having switched off, he hunched himself up in his chair as sullenly as a peevish child.

Unwilling to be fobbed off, Hugo ventured: 'I was thinking it's time we had a progress report. Done anything positive yet?'

Patrick considered. 'You'll find that the plan for impregnating the key sales management has been implemented.' Each word was enunciated with a tinge of mockery. 'Only, as I told you, it was hardly worth the effort. Kids' stuff.' Again he kept Hugo waiting, but there was something he simply had to express. 'Actually, I'm thinking now of something a bit . . . well, you might call it negative. Decisively so. Let me wander.'

'Sorry? I don't get you. I was hoping that after that discussion we had about the Valence campaign, when' — Hugo emphasized — 'we all agreed on directing some carefully calculated hints into — '

'Done,' said Patrick. 'I've already told you that phase one has been implemented.' Again a condescending grin. Then: 'But I've had a more important idea. Disrupting the competition first. Much more effective. Leave some corpses scattered by the wayside, to leave the field clear, as it were.'

'I'm not sure I like the sound of that. Our whole PR philosophy is based on . . . well, persuasion.'

'Yes, yes,' said Patrick impatiently. 'But maybe a bit of something heftier can help things along. Though,' he grinned suddenly, 'it might take some explaining to your rather hidebound clients.'

'How about explaining it to me, for starters?'

'Let me wander,' said Patrick again.

*   *   *

Edgar Seymour of Lauriston Cosmetics was a stocky fifty-year-old, known as a good listener. In board meetings or sales conferences he rarely contributed assertive opinions on general policy or specific campaigns. He had worked his way up in the firm by turning that gaze of his thoughtfully from side to side, biding his time before committing himself to a decision, and gaining a reputation as a solid, reliable character who could be turned to in times of stress when everybody else was at loggerheads.

He had learned, early on, the advantages of staying quiet until everybody else had had their say. Let rival colleagues bluster on, overdoing things, while you regretfully found ways of preparing to tidy up after a collapse.

It had the advantage of being honest. There were few situations in which you couldn't genuinely point out defects, express a few honest reservations, and then, as a loyal member of the team, honourably submit to more powerful recommendations. Let those other men make the mistakes. Watch their enthusiasms. Envy them their certainties, their confident hard-selling techniques. Express a few polite doubts but then defer to them . . . and afterwards, with an apologetic shrug, which was never quite brash enough to say 'I told you so', tidy up their mess and smile that wide, tolerant smile as they acknowledge you'd been right in the first place. He had learned, what so few of the bright boys ever understood, that in aiming for top managerial posts a man will prosper more soundly in big business by recommending ways of not doing things than by going recklessly ahead and forcing them through.

This evening he had decided to go to bed early. He had brought a sheaf of papers home with him, and spent two hours going through them after dinner, but relished the thought of his favourite routine of taking ideas to bed with him and lying awake dictating final recommendations into his old-fashioned bedside recorder.

His wife had gone into her little sitting room to watch television. They had not watched programmes together for a long time now. Nor had he discussed business with her, as he had tried to do in their early years together. It was a relief to drift away from that routine. His careful, logical approach to everything could be disrupted by inexplicably disturbing moments — absurdities that would have surprised those colleagues who regarded him as so solid, stolid, predictable. Such as those times during an evening when his wife would get up from her large leather armchair and say she was going to bed, or was going to have a bath, or simply — and suddenly bitter — was bored and wished he would stop rustling those infernal papers. The back of that armchair had been creased into a threatening grimace: two deep creases for the eyes, a squashed nose, a slack, gloating mouth squeezed into a grin as sour as her pallid lips.

The firm had once sent him to a psychiatrist as part of their staff medical and insurance coverage. He had not told the man about the face in the armchair, or about the recurrent dream that had haunted him since childhood, because, being the man he was, he knew that such things were just as irrational as so many of his colleagues' decisions. They should be kept in their place until he was ready to deal with them — or ignore them as being irrelevant.

They had been kept at bay for many years now.

He had a quick shower and went to bed.

He and his wife had not shared a bed for quite some years, having abandoned futile attempts to produce a child. Edgar Seymour was modest enough to admit that the fault could have been his. Humility was a key element in that cautious philosophy of his. Lecturing staff or manoeuvring his way through executive discussions, his pleasantly offhanded 'Oh, my fault — a bit of an error there' was very disarming. Especially when it turned out that he had been right after all.

He lay down but postponed sleep by dictating the facts he had prepared in favour of Lauriston's takeover of the

Valence company. Their main rival had been aware of the threat for some time now, but had prepared their financial defences well. Mr. Seymour's colleagues had come close to ruining the amalgamation by boasting wildly inflated figures and juggling forecasts too erratically. He must devise a way of blocking young Macklam's brash policy without committing himself to outright condemnation.

He began juggling mentally with figures. It was a good way to keep sleep at bay. He could never be sure that he might not be plagued by that old dream of his.

It all went back to childhood, when he had been accidentally stuck in a cupboard. It was his own fault, and he had admitted it. That had been his way of things from the start. But for once his admission had not led to better things. Repeatedly, at unpredictable times but perhaps related to a stressful moment in school or, supposedly adult, in daytime business negotiations, he would find himself here in this familiar room with everything normal . . . until the walls started closing in on him, squeezing the breath out of him, and the ceiling began to descend to crush him from above. He would wake panting for breath; and reach for some notepad or his dictating machine and soothe his mind with the pleasures of calculation.

One of the office girls had once got herself trapped in the office cupboard by a falling map drawer jamming the door. There had been some suggestive jokes around the department, but Mr Seymour's unforced, genuine sympathy soothed her wonderfully, and she was his slave thereafter.

Tonight he worked until his grasp of the key figures began to slacken. He didn't really want to go to sleep, but his eyes were stinging and there was something scratching at the edges of his mind, like a cat trying to find a way of edging through the narrowest possible opening of a door.

He told himself he was comfortable, in his own bed in his own room. At last he gave way, and slept.

Yet even in the darkness of sleep the contours of the room were still clear. He tried to shut out the vision, but although there was no light on he could still see the wall beyond the foot of the bed, and a face leering out of it at him. A leather wall, creaking. And when he moved on to his left side, wasn't there a shadow of someone leaning towards him, telling him to get up and alter those figures he had so painstakingly calculated?

'No, certainly not.' But then: 'Well, of course one is always open to error. Perhaps if I can have another look . . . '

He was struggling to sit up in bed. But he couldn't make himself move. He was pinned there as the walls began to move in on him. They crunched into the sides of the bed, and the wall at the foot began to tilt towards him, and the ceiling was getting closer and closer. He went on fighting to push his way up, but the bedclothes were pinioning his arms. Then familiar objects began shaking themselves loose — the hairbrush off the dressing table thudding into his right ear, a shower of tissues tearing themselves into shreds in his hair, all familiar things turning against him.

Just as he had always feared, but had been able to conceal from his employers and employees and the firm's hired psychiatrist. But who was this close to him now, listening in, feeling every tremor of his self-awareness and laughing at it?

At the same time columns of figures began racketing round and round in his head, somehow telling him that his only way out was to get these figures back into a completely different sequence and admit that his theories had been wrong.

He could take no more.

'Yes, all right, all right. Let me see . . . just another look . . . if I can just get at my . . . at my . . . '

He was awake, sweat pouring off him. The sheet bunched around his neck was sodden with it. He reached for the light, and then for his recorder. As a child, he had groped for his teddy bear. Now he talked in spasms until nearly dawn, but had as little recollection of what he had recorded as of what he had originally worked out. The only thing clear, even in daylight, was still the nightmare.

He left the house early without waiting

for his wife to come down for breakfast. Gradually he relaxed in the familiar driving seat of his elderly but painstakingly maintained Saab. He had never been one to squander money — his own or the company's — on regular flashy replacements. As he started up, he was uneasy for a moment about the contents of the recorder and briefcase on the seat beside him, but grew in confidence as he slid into gear and the familiar roads opened up before him.

It was always a relaxing twenty minutes between here and the office, even when that stretched to thirty minutes because of vagaries in the morning traffic. He was never impatient. Road rage was for the aggressive, not for Edgar Seymour, who daily intended to reach his destination in one piece.

The Lauriston building was in sight ahead when he put his foot down, approaching a junction where a slip road fed in from the left. Ahead of him an artic had begun swinging into the central lane to allow a builder's truck in from the approach road. The car was going wonderfully smoothly, and he was quite confident of being able to coast through the gap between these other two vehicles.

Yet now, in spite of his foot being hard down, the Saab was slowing. Suddenly there were dark bulks to either side, cutting off the light. From the seat beside him his brief case, which he was used to tucking comfortably under his arm when he strode into the office, was warping, its edges compressed into spikes which drove into his side. He tried to squirm away, but the door was weighing heavily against him from the other side. He let out a brief little moan as his elbows were pinned to his side. His arms held rigid, he desperately tried to turn the wheel a few inches. Since his car had all at once become so narrow, it should surely get through the shrinking space between the truck and the artic.

It was only a dream. Had to be. You just knew it couldn't be real, and any minute you would wake up, sweating and thankful it hadn't been real.

Only this time it was real.

The world was closing crushingly in on

him. Closing so slowly, taking an eternity for the sides of the car to squeeze in and start bringing the blood out, squeezed out from both sides and finally out of his crushed, splintered head.

★ ★ ★

Hugo Lanner folded the morning paper open on the table before him and turned the local news item towards Patrick, waiting for a reaction. There was none. At last Hugo said:

'Is this what you meant? This *was* your doing, wasn't it?'

Patrick went so far as to smile. 'Quite a night,' he said complacently.

'Look, I don't think we ever contemplated — '

'An obstacle has been removed. Quite an important one.'

The death of Edgar Seymour, Marketing Director of Lauriston Cosmetics, had been greeted with shock throughout the trade. First reports of his death in a multiple crash were at a loss to explain how he could have come to drive into an impossibly narrow space between two larger vehicles. His driving record was impeccable. It could only be that he must have lost control of his vehicle because of some mechanical fault or some physical blackout.

His death came at an unfortunate time for his company, which was rumoured to have been involved in a possible takeover bid for one of its major competitors. Documents in the possession of Mr. Seymour would have to be analysed by his fellow directors before any further decisions could be made. In the meantime, there were suggestions that Lauriston's assets might have been over-estimated, and the market would be waiting for a clearer exposition of its viability.

'A useful confusion,' said Patrick. 'Now we can take our time with the wider spread of things.'

Hugo Lanner wanted to say that they none of them wanted to be parties to outright violence — to what might amount to murder. Looking at Patrick, he found he could not phrase his doubts. Or, disquietingly, did not dare to do so.

3

It was a hot day. The sun was drawing the tang of bracken and clover off the moor and mingling it with the flowerbeds around the Burntrigg garden.

The ragged skyline of the building cast a cool shade on the terrace. The three young women taking their midday break made bright splashes of clashing colour against the grey architrave of the high window, which had become a door.

Patrick Robson wheeled himself along the garden path, glancing up occasionally without as much as a smile of recognition.

'Like some grotty teenager,' said Josie McCann, 'wanting to have a go but not knowing how to set about it.'

Bethany Critchley pretended not to hear this. It was not the sort of language she cared to use or to acknowledge. But in this weather it was very much Josie's sort of thinking. She was wearing an outfit that went with the weather, but one

218

Bethany would not have cared to be seen in. The short grey tartan skirt stopped well above Josie's knees, and the flimsy white blouse was open two buttons down. Even in the shade there were sparkling beads of sweat round her neck.

'He's always watching us,' she said.

'I'd say that you're the one who can't take her eyes off *him*,' said Carolyn Finch-Mordaunt.

Josie had in the past remarked — though not to either of them — on the constant unadmitted rivalry between the other two as to which of them could be the most toffee-nosed.

She said: 'What d'you suppose goes on in that mind? It's weird. Sometimes I've had the weirdest dream — '

'Oh, we can just guess what kind of dream,' said Carolyn.

Unexpectedly Bethany said: 'I must admit that sometimes I get a feeling of him being . . . well, snooping. I mean, not so much in a dream as being on edge somewhere, just out of the corner of my eye.'

'Exactly,' said Josie eagerly. 'Like brushing against you, sort of . . . trying you out.'

'Or like someone in a play, behind the curtain, listening.'

'Isn't that something to do with his job?' Carolyn lowered her voice as Patrick progressed slowly below the terrace. 'Something psychological?'

'Or hypnotic. Though Dr. Lanner won't have any talk about that.'

They were silent for a while. They had all had to sign a confidential agreement before starting work here — 'to protect leakages to our competition,' as it was explained to them. But once you had been working closely together for a time, there were questions you couldn't help asking.

Josie could not take her eyes off the young man on his slow, laborious circuit of the garden. You'd have thought he'd have been given a motorized chair to save him all that strain on his arms. Only mightn't he then be tempted to make a swift getaway — down the road to the gate, out and away?

Having completed the circuit he was coming back under the terrace, again glancing up and then looking away.

'Mrs. Storey not taking him for walkies

today?' Josie said mockingly.

'She's gone into town to do some shopping.'

'Surprised one of us didn't get appointed as pusher-of-the-day.'

Carolyn gave a sour little laugh. 'It's ridiculous. Trot him round the grounds, talk to him, put him at ease — but don't ask too many questions. And change the subject if ever he starts talking about dreams. That's a subject reserved for the management.'

'And mustn't go out of the grounds.' Somehow it was resonating in Josie's mind, distracting her from the leisurely warmth of the day.

'He does want to get out of the side gate and down to that stream.' Carolyn shook her head. 'But orders is orders. Not outside the grounds. You'd think he was a toddler, not to be let out of mummy's sight. Or is this a sort of psychiatric hospital we're working in? Sometimes I wonder.'

'We all do,' said Bethany dismissively. 'But we're paid not to ask.' She looked Josie up and down and brusquely changed the subject. 'Doesn't Madam object to you coming in like that?'

Mrs. Saltram liked them to call her Ruth when they were working together; but between themselves they always referred to her as Madam.

'Hasn't said anything.' Josie smirked. 'And Mr. Armour certainly doesn't object.' She was still focussed on Patrick, who had slowed to a halt and was sitting hunched forward as if too tired to push himself any further. 'Supposing one day he grows up and makes a grab for one of us?' When the two of them pointedly ignored her, she added: 'Bags I get first grab.'

Bethany looked even more aloof. Josie envied her that cool manner, while at the same time being exasperated by it. It must inflame quite a few young men, but Bethany was the sort who could pick and choose. Did she ever, Josie wondered enviously, choose?

Bethany and Carolyn both got up and went indoors.

Patrick turned to stare openly up at Josie, as if summoning up the courage to ask her for a dance.

She went down to him and settled her hands on the back of his chair.

★   ★   ★

They moved slowly and steadily towards the gate and looked down through it towards the meandering stream on its way to the Tyne. Without a word Josie opened the gate, and they went through the opening and down the gentle slope.

To one side was a birch plantation with a carpet of thick undergrowth. Josie made a move towards one of the narrow paths weaving its way to one of the shady glades deep inside. But Patrick's hands gripped the wheels, and without a word he had steered them into the bumpy descent towards the stream. It was all a bit open down there for what Josie had in mind, but she took over the steering the way he wanted it.

Then she screamed.

A small grass snake had writhed across her path, almost touching her toes through her open sandals.

'Harmless.' Patrick twisted his neck to glance back. It was the first time he had spoken.

'How would you know?'

He shrugged.

'I'm terrified of snakes,' she confessed sheepishly, but using the excuse to lean forward, shivering, and let her forehead nuzzle his cheek.

Now they had reached the level and she was having to push hard to get on to the spongy grass of the haugh.

In the middle of the tiny promontory thrusting into the curve of the stream was a stone like a squat altar, with a jagged hole through the middle. Patrick raised his right hand commandingly, and Josie found herself heading towards it as if drawn by a magnet. When they reached it, she let go of the metal arms of the chair and collapsed onto the grass, propping herself on her right elbow and easing herself sideways, close to the chair, so that he could see down her cleavage.

He stared at the large hole through the middle of the stone.

She wondered if he was queer, or what

Bethany languidly referred to among her ex-public school friends as a Gneut — the Great English Neuter.

She stretched her right leg out. Not as sleek as Bethany's, all right, but it was pretty tempting all the same, wasn't it?

Without asking for her assistance, Patrick jolted himself as close as he could get to the stone, leaning forward over it with his arms dangling to embrace it. Josie wriggled past him, easing herself round to the other side, and edging her right hand and arm through the hole from the other side.

His head went up. They stared straight into each other's eyes. Josie laughed, and stabbed forward with her hand. Her aim was perfect . . . or had he been knowingly positioning himself, waiting for her? Certainly his body was as wide-awake as those hungry eyes. She laughed again, found it was difficult to stop laughing as she clawed at the belt of his trousers . . . only to find that he was already loosening it, and was breathing in short, rasping spasms as she grasped him.

She realized that he had thrust himself

forward, out of his wheelchair, and was taking all his weight on his arms as he levered himself round the stone. She began heaving herself up to meet him. The stone was hot. Patrick's hand, groping to get a grip on her left arm, was hotter. She caught his hand with her own and steered it, taking all his weight on her body now, while he began wrenching the flimsy blouse from her shoulders.

His hands clawed into her waist, and as his teeth bit into her shoulder he groaned a deep, rhythmic groan.

'Say something, Patrick,' she panted. 'Come on, shout something . . . anything.'

He pushed himself up on his arms and was staring down into her face. Nothing remote about him now. But nothing loving, nor even a grimace of pleasure or surprise at what he was experiencing. The grass was raw and rough beneath her. She wanted to move, but he had pinned her down and was still staring as he poised himself.

'Who are you looking at?' she gasped. 'Christ, Patrick, who d'you think I am?

Who d'you think you're — '

Words dissolved into a howl of pain.

When it was over he rolled over on his side, dragging his slacks awkwardly up again and reaching for the side of his chair. He didn't ask for her help; kept his head turned away and didn't look at her again. The years must have given him a terrific strength in those muscles: bracing his foot against the base of the stone, he gripped the arms of his chair and hauled himself up at a crazy angle and twisted himself round to flop back onto the seat.

The day was still hot, but Josie felt a chill creeping from inside her: not from inside her body, but from the depths of her mind. Wretchedly she pulled her skirt on, made herself sit up, tried to feel triumphant and fulfilled. Well, at least she could claim to have been the one to rob him of his virginity. Something to tell the girls. And then share him around?

Abstractedly he was reaching out towards the hole in the stone, as if to conjure up some phantom creature from within it. Josie made another sudden stab with her hand, reaching through the hole and this time catching his wrist.

'You know what this stone's called?'

'Of course I know.'

'The handfasting stone.' He was trying to pull free, but she held on grimly. 'Well,' she teased wildly, 'are we going to pledge our troth?'

The indifference in his eyes had become flooded with a blaze of anger. Worse. Of outright hatred. In a voice of cold fury such as she had never heard before, from him or from anyone, he said: 'Don't contaminate it. I'm bespoken.'

'Bespoken?' she echoed mockingly. 'Oh, come on, Patrick. You don't mean . . . no, don't tell me . . . Carolyn's already had you down here? She's a sly one. And you.' A nerve began twitching in his left cheek, and his eyes were so frightening that she began babbling, trying to keep it all as a joke. 'Or Bethany? No, I don't see you and Bethany, somehow.'

'Handfasted,' he said, 'to someone far beyond your understanding.'

He wrenched himself free and began turning the chair awkwardly in the grass. Josie stood up and stumbled towards the back of the chair. He tried to escape, but could not push himself fast enough.

'Back to base, right?' She tried to make it light-hearted.

But he twisted his head round to glare up at her and said: 'None of this was meant to happen.'

'They all say that,' she jibed, 'afterwards.'

'I disgust myself. You've . . . contaminated everything.'

'Thanks, I'm sure.'

'I'll give you the chance to release me. Now. And we'll say no more.'

She was so shaken by the seething hatred in every word that all she could think of was to tantalize him, go on making a desperate joke out of it. 'Oh, no.' She thrust the chair as hard as she could up the slope. 'That's not the way the handfasting works. The year's not up. You've got to wait a year and then we both agree to call it a day. Not before.'

'You can't be allowed to come between us.'

'Between . . . between you and . . . sorry, I don't get you.'

'You can't be allowed to block the way.'

The words came out like an incantation. 'We both agree to end the troth now. If we both agree — '

'But we don't. I don't. So you're hooked,' she taunted.

He did not utter another word until they reached the garden and then, over his shoulder, he said: 'It won't do. You must be cancelled out.'

Finally she let him go, and he manoeuvred himself under the terrace and into the lower door of the tower basement.

The other girls, who had seen him arriving, came out on the terrace and waited expectantly for Josie.

Carolyn said: 'You didn't take him *outside?*'

'You going to sneak to Madam?' said Josie.

'Well, no, but . . . I mean, you know we've been told . . . '

Bethany was refusing to show interest. But for once Carolyn could not maintain her pose of detachment. 'Anyway,' she said eagerly, 'what was he like?'

Josie had hoped to boast to them. But

it had all gone sour, and that was something she didn't want to admit to. 'A bit of a creep,' she managed to say. 'A bit clumsy, frankly.'

'That's what I'd have expected, first go,' said Carolyn. 'Going to continue the lessons?'

'I don't think he's very promising material. A bit too weird, really. Full of hatred, in a way.'

'Of himself?' said Bethany in her best worldly-wise tone.

★   ★   ★

Josie was glad to get away from Burntrigg that afternoon. Patrick had not shown up for the rest of the day, for which she was thankful. But she was desperate to turn her back on the place and everything in it. She couldn't imagine how she would face coming back next morning. She ached with a more than physical battering — not just the savagery of Patrick's lovemaking, but the worse assault of his voice.

She felt she was being followed, yet

there was no car behind her. When she had parked the Fiat in the garage round the corner, there was an even stronger sensation of being watched as she walked to the flat — watched from a great distance, from above and all around at the same time.

Watched by something waiting to pounce.

With the door of the flat closed behind her, her first need was for a large vodka and tonic. She managed a second one within ten minutes, and then slumped down on her bed. When her eyes closed, she felt a tumult of shadows rushing in on her. She was terrifyingly sure that she must not let herself go to sleep. Somebody . . . something . . . was waiting for her in the darkness.

She got up, opened the window, switched the television on. When she realized that she had not taken in the slightest item of the programme, she concentrated on making a meal, washing the dishes afterwards, tidying the kitchenette, then having a bath. For once she was temped to leave the bathroom door open; but forced herself to close it.

Until eventually there was nothing else to do but go to bed.

And sleep.

And dream.

They had been waiting. They came at her now from under the bed, from under the bedroom door, from out of the walls. Snakes, sliding across her shoulders and coiling round her neck. A glistening green thing looping itself around her breasts.

She struggled to free herself, twisting and turning in the bed, trying to drag herself up and out on to the floor. But other serpentine coils seized her arms, slithered around her, and then —

'You bastard.'

She screamed it once. Once only, gasping for breath as there seemed to be another tongue swelling in her mouth, a scaly creature sliding in, tasting her, choking her, plunging further and further down, writhing and lashing as it went.

Part Four

DISSONANCES

1

'I've got him,' said Dominic triumphantly, 'coming through loud and clear.'

His lean, hungry face was flushed. He stared at Muir like a dog waiting to be patted and tossed a kind word.

'How?' demanded Muir. 'Where is he?'

'That I can't say . . . yet.'

'You said he was coming through loud and clear.'

'Yes, but it'll take time to establish the exact location. Like radar — or radio-direction-finding.'

'Look, if you got what we might call a signal — '

'Like an explosion in my head,' said Dominic. 'He let loose a whole blast of energy. Uncontrollable. Like someone who's been keeping very quiet for a long time and then blowing his top.'

Muir said: 'All right, what caused it this time? Can it lead us to him?'

'Something very personal — to do with

some girl he'd . . . well, gone for. Went at it hard enough to kill her, I'd say. The sheer intensity of it came right through to me. *En clair.*' He was smirking again.

'Killing someone? If there's anything in the papers, we might get a lead.'

'We can analyse the surroundings.' Dominic was talking to himself. 'He'll have shut down, put up the firewall again. But just for that once he let it all slip, and I might . . .' He could have been listening for a change in wind direction. 'I'm sure I can pick him up again, now he's given us that opening. Get a hint of what he's working on, what his surroundings are, what echoes they leave in his mind during the night.'

'Then for Christ's sake get down to it,' rasped Muir. 'Go to it. Get out there and find him.'

One of the necessary conditions was that Dominic should go to sleep during the day, whenever it suited him.

'While the rest of us,' said Slee resentfully, 'have to stay awake and plod along every minute of the day.'

He was sourly pleased when Dominic's

research slumbers were interrupted by the return of their latest detainee from Morocco. The message from his handlers there was terse and to the point. 'This man is very stubborn. Before returning him to base, you will need to intensify your preparatory treatment.'

Which meant that Dominic's dream researches needed to be switched for the moment to a fiercer, more concentrated torment. Like planting a virus in a computer network, thought Muir. But was the young man up to it? There was something too languid about him: a lazy spitefulness rather than an utter commitment to inducing the terror, which they needed against terrorists.

How could they get their hands on this other polluter of dreams, who sounded as if he had such superior qualifications?

There was another snag, something unforeseen. The subject was no longer complaining about sleep deprivation. Not after last time. He was in no hurry to plunge into a sleep poisoned by Dominic's harrowing implications, second-rate as they might be, and was stubbornly fighting against drowsiness.

'And on top of that,' Slee complained to Muir, 'the layabout himself can't force himself to go to sleep as often as we need. We've tried drugging him to get him off, but then he doesn't seem to function properly.'

'Bloody ridiculous. Ever hear of an operative wearing himself out with too much sleep?'

'That's about the size of it. Some of us,' added Slee dourly, 'wouldn't mind coping with problems like that.'

They fought their way through the usual procedures, but the rendition was not working out the way the controllers in the States would have wanted. The prisoner emerged from his ordeal shaken, but with a defiant attempt to control the twitching of his lips and the wincing at every jolt they imposed on his body prior to returning him to base.

Dominic Lynch looked even more shaken. Back in the safe house, he did not go for his usual lie-down but sat slumped in a chair while Muir had his ritual drink and burst out impatiently: 'All right, lad, let yourself relax. Fine. But you're still on duty, remember. While you're taking a break, let your mind do a recce. Get out there and look around. You've as good as found that other member of your . . . your clan. Keep after him.'

Dominic yawned. His eyes stayed blank until Dr. Sedlák and his daughter drove up and came into the sitting room. Then he looked at Milada and smiled a drowsy smile, inviting a smile in return. She looked down shyly, the light from the window glinting in her hair and coaxing a glow from her bare arms.

Sedlák said: 'You have seen the local gazette?'

Muir grunted a negative.

'But this could be the site.' Sedlák waved the paper at Dominic. 'This could be the workplace, yes? Copsholm Communications — it could be there that you . . . shall we say, visited?'

Dominic sat up, suddenly wide-awake. 'Yes, that's them. Copsholm. That's the name.'

'And who the hell might they be?' demanded Muir. When Sedlák handed him the paper, he skimmed the main column. 'Communications? Public Relations? What would our man be doing with an organization like that?'

'Experts in advertising,' Sedlák suggested. 'Subliminal advertising, perhaps? We have read that your Advertising Standards Authority is growing worried about the way some practitioners are influencing the minds of the public, especially children.' He was toying with concepts that obviously appealed to some deep interests of his own. 'Commercial brands are using loopholes to market directly to minors in digital environments — those networking sites which every child stares at and uses by the hour nowadays. And now that product placement is being legalized in actual feature programmes . . . ' He pursed his lips. 'From a child with, shall we say, an influential father, what influences may be passed upwards and outwards?'

Muir folded the paper impatiently.

'What's this got to do with kids' minds? There's a young woman here who's been found dead, and' — he waved the paper at Dominic — 'you're thinking it's the one you came across being killed?'

'In her dream, yes.'

'Christ, what sort of strain do they put their staff under?'

'It wasn't the employers who put her under strain,' said Dominic. 'It was Patrick . . . yes, that's it, Patrick Robson . . . it was him. I told you. I *felt* him. In a rage. Because — '

'Because he was angry with himself.' Milada was speaking very quietly, looking at something far away. 'He had betrayed our handfasting. I heard him. And the woman who contaminated him. Not far from here. The two of us,' she said raptly, 'close at last.'

Dominic was staring a challenge at her.

'The punishment.' She was quieter than ever, pale and troubled. 'Perhaps he went too far. But that foolish woman had transgressed.'

'Handfasted?' Dominic was impatient, eager to talk to her, oblivious to the rest of them. 'But that lasts for only a year, before either of you decides one way or the other.'

'You know as well as I do' — she was chiding him gently, like an amused older sister — 'that for us time is a different concept.'

It burst out of Dominic. 'You! You're one of *us*.' He went on staring at her raptly. 'One of *us*.'

She smiled demurely.

'Hold on a minute,' snapped Muir. 'Can you just give me some idea what the hell — '

'Yes,' said Sedlák. 'That is true. That is why I was brought here. With my Milada.'

'Damn it, you've never told me this before. I'm supposed to be in charge of operations here, remember? To know everything about my staff. *Need to know* — the rules are clear enough.'

'It was agreed I should bring Milada here.' Sedlák pursed his lips condescendingly. 'But she is not to be used until she is mature enough to cope with those problems I have spoken of. She is not to be rushed. Or exploited.'

Muir decided it was time to pull rank. 'Since you've been told to bring her here, she comes under my command. She'll be used any way I decide. When it's an operational necessity.' An uneasy thought occurred to him. 'You, Professor: are you one of them yourself? One of these oddballs?'

Sedlák shook his head. 'My late wife was a Moravian. From Cejkovice, a little village in the vineyards of the Moravske-Slovensko. They have their old traditions, their own customs and mysteries, the wine-growers down there.'

'After a bottle or two, no doubt.'

'My wife was the one from whose powers came Milada's powers also. And I repeat — she will be subject to no orders and will take no actions until she is ready.'

Dominic still had not taken his eyes off Milada. 'The two of us together! What we might achieve!'

'Damn right,' growled Muir. 'The two of you can put your heads together, or go to sleep together, any which way, but find that bloody man. What d'you say his name is?'

'Patrick,' said Milada dreamily. 'Patrick Robson.' She looked at her father. 'I think it is time I went to him.'

He said nothing, but his sombre gaze took in Muir and Dominic Lynch before turning to Muir with what might almost have been an accusation of personal guilt.

'Perhaps theirs is not such a valuable gift. How long can young people like this make free of other folks' dreams without themselves being . . . how shall I put it . . . infected? They plant ideas, some of them poisonous. How can one be sure these poisons do not flow back into their own minds and fester there? Exposure to the mental sickness and fears of others — it can become a contagion seeping into their own bloodstream.'

'We all have to take the chance of getting wounded in a war,' said Muir. He swung towards Dominic. 'Right, young man. Back to business. For the last time, just how are you going to lure this Robson character over here?'

It was Milada who answered, keeping an eye on Dominic as she did so, seeming to wait on his confirmation. 'The place where he works, they need a replacement for the girl he destroyed. Yes?'

Dominic nodded. 'They'll be wanting a

computer operator, yes.'

'Plant her there,' barked Muir. 'And we get our communications direct from within. You'll draw him out, young lady, keep us in touch . . . and show us the exact moment when we can lure him out.'

Milada looked apologetically at her father. 'I think I am ready. I think it is time I went to him,' she said again, and quietly added: 'For his own sake.'

'And bring him here,' Muir insisted.

'You know how to get there?' Dr. Sedlák was reluctantly surrendering.

Milada smiled. 'I have never felt him so close.'

2

Bethany Critchley took the notes and figures Ruth had given her and sat down at the computer desk. Her usually carefully tinted face looked grey and puffy. Her whole body twitched every now and then. She could have regarded this routine job as beneath her, to be carried out only in a temporary capacity. From her own long past experiences Ruth understood the hierarchy. Bethany had probably started using computers with a previous firm, when this was the pinnacle of office achievement. It had taken so few years to become everybody's run-of-the-mill chore. Bethany had graduated above that now, but today was resolved to cope, in spite of the after-shock of what she had gone through the previous day.

They would have to hire somebody else to replace Josie. And quickly.

In the meantime there was the report and an imposing set of figures to be communicated to Roger Snape of Valence via his confidential email address.

Half-an-hour into the day, Bethany was offered an unwelcome break.

A police car had arrived at the main entrance to Burntrigg. Matthew Armour was first at the door, wearing a suitably grave and cooperative expression. 'About poor Josie. Yes, of course, officer. We were expecting some inquiries.'

He ushered the Detective Chief Inspector and his constable into the conference room. Ruth hurried to join them, not so much to display a mutual readiness to assist the police in their inquiries as to keep an eye on Matthew and steer him away from any blundering indiscretions.

DCI Ridley formally introduced himself and his DC Malia, a young woman with a notebook, which she appeared to regard with the same distaste as Bethany regarded her screen and keyboard. Then he intoned an explanation of his presence in a voice that managed to be neither suspicious nor easygoing. He was waiting to make up his mind about these possible witnesses, thought Ruth: whether to detect a possible involvement, or whether to write them off as soon as possible. He paused before proceeding, part of his technique to unsettle people.

Matthew fidgeted, just as Ruth had feared he might.

The DCI said: 'I'm sorry to break in on your working day, but we're trying to establish the cause of death of a Miss Josephine McCann of 22A Aysdon House, Heddleton.'

'Poor Josie,' said Matthew.

'She was a regular employee here?'

'She was.'

'When did you hear about her death? And how?'

Ruth said: 'When Josie didn't show up for work next day, we were worried. She was usually a good timekeeper.'

'You say 'next day'. This would be . . . ?'

'The Thursday. After . . . '

'Yes?'

Matthew blurted out: 'One of our staff spent some time with her on the Wednesday, but he didn't notice anything abnormal.'

'One of your staff? May I see her — or him?'

When Matthew opened the door there

was the distant sound of discordant, tangled music from up the stairwell, abruptly cut short, and then an outraged yelp. 'You can't cut it short just like that. Unresolved, you *can't* . . . '

Hugo appeared, pushing Patrick in his chair. Ruth tried to size up what the detective might make of the two of them, wondering for a moment if it might look too much as if Hugo was Patrick's keeper.

There was a flurry of introductions. Patrick was, mercifully, cool. Yes, Josie had taken him for a stroll in the lunch break. They had just been chatting. 'We often do . . . that is,' he said with a convincingly sad dip of his head, 'we *did*.'

'And did she show any signs of stress? About her job?'

'None at all.'

'We've had experience ourselves of computers causing stress.' Ridley turned to Ruth. 'Not just repetitive strain, the usual physical stress. Can bring about considerable mental strain as well.'

'We had no indication of anything like that. She seemed perfectly normal, her usual self. Until . . . '

'Yes?'

'When she didn't show up for work Thursday morning, we tried to contact her. There was no answer on her phone. Or on her mobile.'

'You always kept tabs on your staff?'

'We've always treated them like a family,' Matthew intervened. 'A very happy family, too. Until now.'

'And when you got no reply to your calls?'

'I asked one of Josie's colleagues to drive into town and see if she was ill,' said Ruth.

The DCI glanced at Patrick. 'This . . . Mr. Robson?' He was focusing on the wheel-chair.

'Of course not. One of the girls. A close friend. The one who reported the death. Well, that is, she reported to *you* — to the police — not being able to get in, and waited until your people came and broke in. And . . . found Josie.'

'Of course. And would *she* be on the premises today, this colleague?'

Matthew scurried off to fetch Bethany.

While they were waiting, Ridley abruptly said to Patrick: 'You hadn't had any sort of disagreement? A lover's tiff, that sort of thing?'

'No.' Patrick was icily calm. 'There was nothing like that. In my situation' — he let his arms dangle above the wheels — 'you can see for yourself. We weren't . . . we were just casual friends.'

Bethany arrived. Yes, she had been the one to find Josie, along with two police officers.

'And can you tell us exactly what you *did* find?'

'Do I have to?'

'Perhaps it would be better if I interviewed you on your own.'

'No,' said Bethany quickly. 'No, there's nothing I can't . . . I mean, I've already told Mrs. Saltram how I . . . what I . . . ' Her usual lofty calm had deserted her. 'It was horrible.'

Ridley jerked his head at his constable, who flipped open a page of her notebook and handed it to him.

'Yes, I see.' He took his time over it. 'Must have been a shock to you. These contortions — '

'She was . . . twisted up. With one of

253

the bed sheets rammed in . . . as if she was trying to eat the end of it — twisted into a knot and pushed into her mouth. It must have . . . she must have . . . '

'Officer,' said Ruth, 'do you have to put Miss Critchley through all this? The policemen who helped her get into the flat must have given you all the details. I see no need for her to be forced to go through it all over again.'

Matthew tried to assert himself as well. 'We don't want another member of staff collapsing.'

'I don't think there's anything more you can tell us,' Ridley conceded. 'We just had to check the whole background. A nasty business for all of you. The police surgeon and a local GP agree that the symptoms could be those of an epileptic fit. But how she got tangled up with those sheets . . . ' He grimaced at Bethany. 'Sorry you had to be there. But thank you for your cooperation.'

'What about her family?' asked Ruth. 'I think we have an address somewhere for her mother and father — '

'In Carlisle, yes.' The constable was

closing her notebook. 'We found their address and phone number in the flat.'

'And the epilepsy? Had there been anything like it before? We certainly never saw any symptoms while she was working here.'

'The parents say the same. Never been any sign of it. No history of it in the family.' Ridley got up. 'Thank you for your cooperation,' he said.

As the police car drove away, Bethany turned towards Patrick as if to fire a question at him. But his polite attentiveness to the detective had drifted back into a defiant blankness, and without a word he began pushing himself towards the stairs.

Matthew said: 'Just a minute. You sure there wasn't something about Josie you didn't tell them?'

'Such as?'

'I don't know. But if there's something you ought to tell *us* . . . I mean, was there something you did notice, after all? When she took you out for that walk with her. Must have been some sort of indication, eh?'

Patrick stopped for a moment at the door.

'She's been cancelled out,' he said coolly.

As they heard the stairlift very softly going upstairs, Matthew said: 'I don't like it. All right, he's making himself useful to us, but I can't feel comfortable with him. I get this feeling of him . . . well, waiting, all set for when he . . . well, like a time bomb ready to explode when — '

'When what?' growled Hugo.

'That's what I can't guess. Wish I could, before it's too late.'

* * *

The heat had been oppressive throughout the morning, and early in the afternoon the sky turned a sullen copper colour. Ruth and Bethany worked together to finalize the progress report for Mr. Snape, and stopped for a brief tea break just as the rain started.

'You feel all right?' Ruth studied Bethany at the end of the afternoon. 'You need a few days off, when we've wrapped this business up?'

Bethany managed a smile. 'Thanks, Ruth, but I'm fine. It was pretty ghastly, but I can cope.'

'Great. Call it a day, now. And drive carefully. There'll be some nasty patches between here and the crossroads.'

She had just poured herself a large gin and tonic when Hugo came in. With a lift of the eyebrow in the direction of the corner cabinet he silently suggested he was prepared to join her. They both sat well back in the armchairs as he put his Islay malt and water on the little table near his right elbow, and Ruth let out a long sigh.

As if in answer, there was an abrupt hiss of rain against the window.

Matthew put his head round the door. 'I'm just off.' He glanced at Ruth. 'Staying on?'

'Till the rain stops.'

'Ah.' His gaze wandered speculatively between them. 'Could go on all night.'

'Drive carefully,' said Ruth.

Quite some minutes after Matthew had left, Hugo said: 'He's right, you know.

That rain's not going to ease off.' He had put his glass down. 'You don't want to drive home after a day like this.' His voice had become warm and companionable. 'Why not spend the night here? I could always fit you in.'

'I'm a pretty restless sleeper sometimes.'

'Look, Ruth, we've known one another a long time. Perhaps it's time we got to know one another even better.'

She found she was vaguely contemplating just that, then she shook herself, took a good gulp of her drink, and laughed. 'You creep, Hugo. You're wondering, if we sleep together . . . really *sleep*, that is, before or after we've . . . well, anyway, it's an experiment, isn't it? Wondering if Patrick will come moseying into our mutual dreams?'

'It was only a suggestion. No need to — '

'Yes, very suggestive. But sorry, Hugo, I'm not prepared to be in the guinea pig category.'

She was not sure whether he was disappointed or mildly relieved.

The buzzer of the front door bell startled both of them.

Hugo got to his feet and went out.

A moment later, he was back. 'There's a girl I've steered into reception. God knows how she got here. Says she's looking to fill that job vacancy of ours.'

'But we haven't been advertising it. Haven't even started asking around yet.'

Ruth followed him back into reception. A girl in a dark blue raincoat was standing there, shyly inclining her head.

'I am Milada Sedláková. I am fully qualified as a computer operator. And used to working in strict confidence.'

'But how did you hear about the job?' Ruth fumbled for words. 'And . . . well, I mean, at this time of the evening . . . '

She had heard no sound of the stairlift or the usual slight squeak of approaching wheels, but Patrick was all at once in the room and staring, rapt, at the newcomer.

'It's all right,' he said. 'I sent for her.'

3

The summer seemed to have no end. Even with windows and the terrace door open, meetings were held in a warmth that made concentration difficult. Only Patrick and the newcomer seemed quite content; but were they, wondered Ruth uneasily, paying enough attention to the discussion on the current programme?

'Just to bring you right into the picture.' Hugo had started the morning with a patronizing smile at the young woman who sat so demurely beside Patrick. 'Time you sat in and discovered how we integrate our normal business approaches with the — ah, what shall we call it? — special talents of our star performer. To which I understand you have been contributing in your — um — unique partnership.'

Patrick offered no acknowledgment, even when Milada looked at him fondly. The illustrious Dr. Lanner could rarely before have witnessed a protégé show signs of taking control of a whole situation.

Immediately after her arrival, Milada had moved into Patrick's suite in the turret. There had been no formal request for this, no discussion: it had simply been taken for granted. Even the disgruntled Matthew had not been given time to raise any objection. With equal smoothness Milada had integrated herself with the everyday routine of the team. Patrick's intermittently prickly moments in the past seemed to have been overcome by this addition to his personal well-being.

Already Milada had proved that she could handle the computer, needing almost no instructions on the company passwords or the way Matthew fussily required their reports to be laid out. Patrick's casual shrug had suggested that everyone ought to have taken this smooth transition for granted.

Why then, Ruth fretted, did she keep getting this feeling of insecurity — of a possible infiltration of Copsholm's jealously guarded secrets?

Worse was the creepier sense of these modern infiltrators being not just mere business competitors, but something utterly alien.

'Perhaps today we could discuss a test case,' she ventured. 'This local campaign against the purchase of woodland on the western edge of Simonsyke for development under a PFI scheme. The opponents have come to us through the good offices of a contact in the Council offices, wanting to know how to organize opposition before it's too late.'

'Can they afford us?' asked Matthew.

'Hardly worth calling it a campaign,' said Patrick. 'Simply filling in time until something more challenging comes along. Speaking of which, our friends at Valence are brewing up some more ambitious plans at the moment.'

Matthew glared. 'Where did you learn that? Or are you guessing at something?'

'I never waste time guessing.'

'Now look, lad. If you're going to go on working with us, you've got to play it straight. If you've heard something, then where did you — '

'We don't have to ask that question,' Hugo interrupted.

But he was waiting for an answer.

'A piano,' said Patrick out of the blue. 'We've got to have a piano. Upstairs.'

Matthew snorted. 'That would take some doing. Trying to get a piano up there past that stairlift . . . '

'We need a piano. It's a priority. More important than all this trivia. Milada used to play.'

Ruth looked at the girl and forced an expression of interest. 'You're keen on music?'

'I was not very good.'

'She will play well,' said Patrick, 'when I teach her.'

'Oh, for Christ's sake,' grunted Matthew.

Hugo glared a warning at him and said: 'We can probably get our hands on a small keyboard and — '

'A full-size piano,' Patrick insisted. 'I will compose music for us to play.'

Matthew was not to be silenced. 'And doubtless we'll be supposed to supply a few reams of music paper, or whatever they call it, as well.'

'There'll be no need. I will create it, and it will exist in eternity. Last forever in the eternity of a dreamworld beyond this time-bound everyday world. It will go to the ends of the universe and back and will never need to be written down. It will be there to be picked up by everyone who wishes to hear and understand it.'

Hugo was leaning forward with his most intense expression. Ruth felt that he longed at this moment to write things down for an addition to his voluminous case files later. 'A sort of universal downloading?'

'Speaking of which,' said Ruth, 'we really do need to concentrate on our approach to one or other of these projects before us. That, in case you've forgotten, is what we're here for.' Reluctantly she consulted Patrick. 'What's this rumour you've picked up? We're in Valence's good books right now. We can probably stall on anybody else. Keep them waiting. Or maybe tackle two or three at a time, with our present staff.' She felt as guilty about the flattery as Hugo had looked earlier.

'The House of Valence' — Patrick made it mockingly resonant — 'is a new name for their joint venture with a developer. Planning to open twenty luxury goods stores a year over the next six years. Each one featuring a self-contained classier boutique with limited access.'

'Limited, no doubt,' said Hugo, 'to those who can afford it. Carefully screened, implying it's a privilege to be allowed to enter. Nothing like putting minor restrictions in place to bring the gullible ones clamouring for admission.'

'And our part in all this?' Matthew demanded. 'Since you know so bloody much, I suppose you've got it all figured out.'

Milada cast a long look at Patrick, as if seeking his approval, then said: 'Of course we continue promoting the company's products. But also we advise on staffing. We make the choice of men and women right for the job, and make sure they are well treated. Good for them, and good for the customers.'

'Get rid of that trumped-up little sod Snape for starters?' Matthew made an exaggerated wave of his arms at the ceiling. 'Bastard should be hanged. Then drawn and quartered!'

'We will be the ones to guarantee trouble-free working conditions,' Milada emphasized, 'as part of the commitment.'

'That'd be a tough full-time job on its own, though. Can't have one of us whizzing between premises all day and every day. And the present bosses aren't going to opt out of all responsibility without a struggle.'

'None of us has to be physically present,' said Patrick. 'They'll not be aware of us. Shareholders' meetings will go on as usual, and board meetings the same, but meaning even less than usual. There are three men and a woman at the top who'll have to be programmed; but with the certainty of large bonuses for them if we're left to our own devices, they aren't going to argue.'

'We make it all so happy,' said Milada.

Her head turned again towards Patrick. Like a ventriloquist's dummy? Ruth shifted uneasily.

'Wasn't there something else to be discussed?' Matthew's voice was resentful.

'Something that was actually on the agenda?'

Ruth turned over the sheets in front of her. 'We have been approached in strict confidence by a local councillor to advise on building a wind farm above Millsyke. It's a scheme opposed by a majority on the council, and by a vigorous public campaign. But important financial interests are involved.'

'Interests of certain councillors?' said Hugo.

'There are certain other interests to be overcome. One or two equally important councillors are asking awkward questions.'

'Why not go over all their heads?' said Patrick. 'Find someone in Whitehall, in the Department of Town and Country Planning. Or go straight for a Minister who needs funding to reinforce the battlements of his country house.'

'We're really getting ambitious now, aren't we?' Today Matthew seemed determined to play the part of devil's advocate.

'It's time we did become more ambitious. We need to stretch ourselves. Work at full capacity.'

Patrick was looking at Milada, silently

267

demanding her support. She said: 'Yes, once we have made the contact, we can move in and . . . coax them.' Ruth was struck by the sexual force behind that emphasis on the word 'coax'.

'No,' said Patrick. 'Here we do not coax. We frighten. Always more effective. More creative. And a lot more enjoyable.' He was talking to himself rather than anybody in this room. 'Pain and pleasure — they're so intermingled. I feel the absolute beauty of pain as I inflict it. That's the difference between Dominic Lynch and myself. Why he will never make the breakthrough.'

Milada lowered her eyes, and Ruth saw that her fingers were twitching until she clasped her hands together to control them. 'Now you make it sound too much like those people my father has been working with. This is why they wanted me to bring you to them. It is not the way we should look at problems. I thought we agreed — '

'We talk about this later,' said Patrick.

The chink of cups and saucers announced that Mrs. Storey had decided this was the time for the tea break. She wheeled her trolley in, looked stonily at Milada, and smiled at Patrick.

It was the first time that Ruth had noticed how Mrs. Storey had smartened herself up; or, rather, softened herself. She no longer had the trim starchiness of a professional nurse. Her attentiveness to Patrick's needs when he first came to Burntrigg had been professional and uncomplaining. But since the arrival of 'that young woman', as Ruth had once overheard her call the new arrival in a brief conversation with Bethany, she was becoming less subservient.

Competing with the young Milada in Patrick's eyes? Competing as a woman? Absurd!

They watched silently as Mrs. Storey poured the tea and coffee. She regarded it as an essential part of her duties to go through this ritual. She took longer over Patrick's cup than over the others. When it came to Milada she hesitated again, but this time not so much offering milk and sugar as daring the girl to make a request.

When Mrs. Storey had gone, Matthew

said: 'We've got to make a decision. The Valence stores, or the wind farm over the moor there?'

Hugo said earnestly: 'We need to assess this new possibility. Let's leave it over until tomorrow. Sleep on it.' His attempt at a sort of roguish smile at Milada struck Ruth as being way out of character. 'You know, sometimes I wish I could be a little bird on a bough in one of your dreams. Cut a lot of corners that way, hm?'

'Perhaps one day they may join us?' Milada consulted Patrick. 'It is true, it could often save time explaining things next day.'

Ruth shivered for a moment, wondering just how an outsider would cope, being drawn into the mesh of those two minds.

Patrick's response was, without a word, to turn his chair ninety degrees. It could be a signal. Or a command. He no longer needed to grip the wheels of his chair and propel himself towards the stairlift. Milada pushed him, every now and then bending forward and whispering something inaudible to anyone nearby.

When they had heard the lift start up, and could visualize Milada climbing the stairs a few steps behind it, Matthew heaved himself to his feet. 'I suppose *somebody's* got to put up a pretence of doing a day's work.'

After he had gone back to his office, Ruth turned to Hugo. 'Aren't you worried about this whole situation? I mean . . . well, the way things are building up between that young couple?'

'It's early days. I think it's going to be quite exciting. It's clear that the two of them are capable of pooling resources. The results could be to make Patrick's powers more than double their intensity. Their joint powers . . . it could be quite awe-inspiring.'

'Provided they're under control.'

'Yes.' Hugo stretched his legs out and contemplated his impeccable shoes for reassurance. 'Under *our* control.'

'And provided we can keep them that way. We don't know whether that girl's influence is going to be good or bad. She looks innocent, but how much do we know about her background?'

'Patrick is satisfied.'

Very much so, thought Ruth, who was far from satisfied. When she had tried, a few days after Milada's arrival, to sound Patrick out as amiably as possible, he had brushed questions aside. 'She's here. I need her here. You need her as well. I'll be responsible for her.' And before she could find a way of asking how the girl had been able to fit so competently into the entire Copsholm routine, he had added: 'You can be sure that she'll do what I want her to do.'

That night, with the soothing buzz of town traffic under her open window, she lay awake for half an hour, then drifted off into sleep which slowly, uncontrollably, became more vivid than day.

* * *

The sounds were no longer those of cars slowing for the traffic lights at the crossroads, or accelerating sharply as the lights changed. Instead she was wandering through a woodland which seemed vaguely familiar but had a path twisting more frequently than she remembered. Then, abruptly, she was in a small clearing, waiting. She had no idea what she was waiting for. Until gradually there was superimposed on the background of trees a sketch of a bedroom, and transparent figures of Patrick and Milada were looking at her from their bed. She tried to stutter an excuse for being there, but immediately they turned their backs and Patrick was hunched over Milada's body, seeming to strike a fist into her naked shoulders in a non-stop pounding. Then he was laughing, and turning her towards him, and their bodies thrashed madly together.

Ruth tried to look away. She hadn't consciously wanted to be an intruder. She refused to be coerced into watching.

Whose dream was this, anyway?

It could be a follow-up of Milada's vague invitation earlier that day, or a trick of Patrick's. More like him than Milada, to invade Ruth's dreams rather than allow her into theirs. But she couldn't believe that her own unaided imagination could have conjured up this picture.

A picture that changed swiftly and

smoothly. She was back in the woodland, but now Patrick and Milada were leaving their bed to join her. As if they had only just become aware of a third party in the room, they got up and within a matter of seconds were strolling along the path ahead of her. Music swelled up from nowhere as they walked. Milada began humming a tune, hanging in the air like a gentle breath of wind through an Aeolian harp . . . until Patrick snarled something, and the fragile beauty became perverted, as if that breath had turned foul, jangling a dissonant music which malevolently twisted the landscape through which they had been walking into something stony and hostile — jagged rocks limned with sour green stripes of lichen, echoing with grating derision. At the far end of the ragged causeway a weird red glow suffused a smoother stone on its promontory in the stream.

Ruth recognized the stone, but was given no time to find it reassuring. Patrick had stopped and turned back towards her, flagrantly acknowledging her presence. He raised his right arm and waved it jubilantly towards the copse to their right. Her feet were somehow trapped. She wanted to escape, right out of this dream, back into her own dream or even better into dreamless slumber or wakefulness. The grip on her was relentless. She was spun slowly round to face the copse.

A man was hanging from a birch tree, swinging slowly to and fro, eyes popping, tongue lolling out. A gagging, retching noise swilled over the music and drowned it.

Rancid green light on the face showed it to be Matthew Armour's.

'No.' Ruth struggled to force words out. 'I won't watch. I don't know what you're trying to prove. It's foul. Stop. Stop now.' Her throat was tightening. Each sound was an agony, until she could no longer force another syllable out.

At the same time Matthew's choking miseries went silent.

'That's better,' Patrick laughed. 'So much better when they're silent. Trying to scream. So much more excruciating for them if they're unable to cry out. Don't you find that?'

Petrified, speechless, she was forced to watch as three men emerged from the shadows. 'You see,' Patrick's voice was boasting somewhere above and behind her although he was still standing there in front of her, gloating. 'They come when I call. Out of their own dreams into a much more enjoyable one.' Moving to the rhythm of his incantations, the men spread Matthew across the fallen bole of a tree and tore his clothes aside. Two of them held him down while the third poised what looked like a scimitar above his bared stomach, waited an interminable moment, then drove it down and began the evisceration.

'Hanged, drawn and quartered, eh?' cried Patrick. 'You've been wondering how to get rid of him, haven't you? How about *this*?' Ruth struggled to look away. She wasn't allowed to. Patrick was provoking her: 'If you want to put him out of his misery, you can kill him now. This very moment. Are you up to it?'

She became aware of some force trying to help her. As her gaze was dragged slowly from the steaming horror of the spectacle, she felt rather than saw Milada moving between her and Patrick. Milada was willing her towards escape, but was herself having to struggle against Patrick, whose anger was unleashing a frenzy of disembodied malice swirling around like a cloud of venomous insects.

Ruth began to run. She was sure this had to be the familiar path that led to Burntrigg. For a moment she stumbled, terrified that someone was poised to stop her.

A shadow moved between the trees, not part of the woodland but somehow detached from it, floating in the air as if any puff of wind might flick it away just as it was howling that discord through the invisible harp: a grey phantom, impossible to bring into focus.

She swerved past it, running so slowly, so heavily, wretchedly slowly.

And was free.

*   *   *

She woke in the early dawn and lay in bed no longer comfortable. She reached for a glass of water, dribbling most of it on the pillow. Then she groped for the bedside phone and dialled a familiar number.

The sleepy grumble was what she might have expected. 'What sort of time d'you call this?'

'Matthew, I just wanted to check.'

'Check what — at this time of the morning?'

'I wanted to be sure you're all right.'

'All right? Christ, why shouldn't I be all right?'

'You haven't . . . had a dream?'

There was a moment's silence. Then he said, 'What sort of dreams I have are my own business,' and rang off.

On the way in to Burntrigg she kept glancing in her mirror and from side to side so make sure the surroundings were as they should be, as one would do if there had been warnings of sudden snowstorms or freakish falls of volcanic ash from some distant eruption. In her tense, twitchy mood she could almost believe that she was being followed — that a large green Volvo was on her tail, edging forward and then falling back again, turning as she turned, going past her at the crossroads but slowing as if considering whether to do a U-turn and pick up the trail again. She shook it off as part of the dream she was trying to shake off.

Indoors Milada was already at the computer keyboard, recording a batch of routine PR jobs. She looked up with a flush of embarrassed recognition. Of course, they had met only a few hours ago.

Matthew came in with a fresh batch of material, glared at both of them as if daring them to question him about the night before, and scurried away.

Like most dreams, last night's should fade quickly, Ruth assured herself. You only remember scattered fragments early in the morning, and by the middle of the day only a muddle of absurdity remains. That was the way it was going to be with this one. Only this one hadn't been remotely like any of the others she could half remember.

One thing she still carried with her was a last-minute vision of Milada in the clearing, spreading her arms as if in a blessing as she freed Ruth from the spell. And it was all so clear that something else was becoming alarmingly clear.

She went to see Hugo.

'I'm still not happy about those two.'

He sighed. 'Aren't you getting twitchy over nothing? I think they're settling in remarkably well. And the girl is more qualified to play a full part alongside Patrick than we dared hope. Give them some breathing space, Ruth.'

'Isn't there a danger of them proving altogether too good? Undermining us, taking over the firm — *our* firm — for their own purposes? Or, rather, Patrick's purposes.'

'And what would those be?'

'I wish I knew. Or,' said Ruth shakily, 'maybe I'm scared of knowing. But' — she took a deep breath — 'one thing I *have* just become aware of.'

'Which is?'

'The girl is pregnant.'

Hugo's reaction might have been querulous or derisive. Instead, he whistled, swayed gently to and fro, and at last said: 'What a fascinating prospect. A child of two of the Gifted Ones. The possibilities . . . '

Yes, thought Ruth. The possibilities. What sort of child would this coupling of the two of them produce — one gifted or cursed?

4

The meeting in London had not been a friendly one. Brigadier Muir came away after a miserable hour from that secluded little room where he had been subjected to what could only be described as a verbal pistol-whipping. And always there was the suspicion of that un-attributable section of the Joint Intelligence Committee nosing its way into field operations while virtuously denying any such involvement.

One thing was made clear. As far as the JIC was concerned, the buck did not stop with them. It was passed expertly down. Muir was determined that it wasn't going to stop with him either. By the time he got back to his own secluded domain in Prestwick he had loaded the ammunition for his own assault, using less subtle language than the convoluted questions to which he had been subjected.

'What the bloody hell happened with

that Glasgow bomber we were supposed to flay into naming his pals?'

'I did have my doubts at the time,' said Slee. 'I did think that maybe he didn't actually have any co-conspirators, and — '

'You weren't asked to think any such thing. It was our brief to come up with names. And the moment my back's turned you let a feeble report go through and chuck the bastard back into the freezer. If I'd known — '

'I left a full report on your desk, sir,' said Slee defensively. 'It made it perfectly clear that Lynch here was unsuccessful in penetrating the suspect's mental defences, and that other tactics would have to be applied. Tactics outside our official remit.'

'Don't tell me. This country does not approve of torture. I must not be told of any breaches of that.' Muir realized that he was echoing the blandly evasive attitude of the JIC. With a splutter of disgust he turned his fury on Dominic Lynch. 'And *you* — what the blazes has got into you? Or more likely drained out of you? Getting too bloody couldn't-care-less?'

Dominic shivered only faintly under the

onslaught, more with distaste than fear. 'I was under pressure to do two things at once.'

'And didn't get a damn thing out of either of them.' Muir switched in an instant from one topic to another. 'Just what excuse have you got for not getting a word back from our Robson character?'

'I've been blocked. It's very tiring, trying to get through.'

'Tiring? And what's this blocked business? I thought the whole idea was to keep in touch through that girl. Easy, you thought. So what's the excuse this time?'

'She's . . . not transmitting. They've combined to shut me out,' said Dominic. 'They've put up a mutual firewall I just can't get through.'

'You mean she's ratted on us? Gone over to them?'

'Something has happened, yes.' He was not apologizing now. His eyes were wide and querulous, seeing or trying to see things beyond the grasp of the others in the room or perhaps even trying not to see them. 'There's something very power-ful between them.'

'So we've been tricked. Played into their hands. Pity you weren't wise to that possibility from the start.' Muir swung back to Slee. 'Since you're the one for applying . . . how did you put it? — 'other tactics' . . . what sort of approach d'you recommend now? A direct assault? Storming the premises of those advertising merchants?'

'If you have the authority, sir, something like that wouldn't actually be impossible. Bring some official pressure to bear. Find some excuse for getting a warrant — '

'Working along with some thick local coppers? Have to do better than that.'

'Actually, I don't suppose a sort of sixteenth-century type raid on Burntrigg would go down too well. Bags of publicity, but not the sort we want. But surely there's something official . . . Defence of the Realm Act, that sort of thing.'

'Our friends in MI6 and the CIA don't like anything as straightforward as that.'

Slee said impatiently: 'OK, what about finding a nice quiet way of kidnapping, no publicity — '

'No,' said Dominic quietly.

'Oh, we're still awake, are we?' said Muir. 'And what might you suggest?'

'Be patient.'

'Patient? I've been kept waiting too bloody long already. Look, let's get down to it. About this firewall, as you call it. There has to be a way of getting through. Or round it. D'you need to get closer — is that the problem?' He brightened for a moment, 'Is there any reason why you shouldn't simply call on them? Walk into that building the way that Milada girl did? Get in and stir things up. And then let us know what the options are, right?'

'Close quarters?' said Slee sceptically. 'Hand-to-hand fighting?'

Dominic yawned. 'I'm tired.'

*   *   *

When Lynch had gone for his usual recuperative lie-down, Professor Sedlák said: 'That poor young man. The strain is telling. So like a vampire, yes? In daytime he is — how you say it? — washed out.'

'All the more reason for fresh blood,' grunted Muir. 'And while we're on the subject of our little washout, how d'you explain that girl of yours not getting through to us? That *was* the idea, wasn't it? What the hell is she up to?'

'You must give her time. I did warn you she ought not to be rushed.'

'Time? Bloody weeks now. You ought to have gone with her that night.'

'You think I would have been made welcome? Come now, Brigadier, it is all too complicated. You must be patient.'

'If I hear that word just once more I'll . . . damn it, while we hang about here, just what . . . how do I get my hands on something . . . *anything?*' Muir clenched his fists. 'She's your daughter. You must have *some* notion how her mind works. She went off willingly enough. I thought she was all set to help us.'

Sedlák said reluctantly: 'I am thinking perhaps her fantasy was real, after all. The handfasting.'

'The what?'

'The troth. Your local tradition of the handfast betrothal. My Milada knew of it before I ever brought her here. She knew of it when she was very little. I used to think it was a childhood fantasy. That was before I learned of her own secret talent within dreams. And now I suspect that she and this Patrick Robson — '

'You mean that instead of acting as our mole, she's ratted on us? A cunning little schemer who's now teamed up with her new boyfriend?'

There was a faint draught as the door opened and Dominic came back into the room, rubbing his eyes as if still trying to wake up.

He said: 'There are things happening.'

'About time too.' Muir waited a moment, then barked: 'All right, let's have it. *What's* happening?'

'There's a disturbance. I can hear . . . feel . . . echoes. Vibrations. *Discords.* Something's about to . . . open up.'

'That's the best you can do?'

'It could be dangerous.' Dominic reached for the arm of a chair and sank into it, exhausted. 'Very dangerous.'

Sedlák got to his feet. 'I do not wish my daughter to be in a danger she may not comprehend. I must go to her.'

'Now you're talking,' said Muir. 'And

while you're there, get some idea of just what our Robson friend is up to. We'll organize some discreet back-up for you and — '

'No,' said Sedlák. 'I go alone.'

★   ★   ★

A light breeze sent a few dry brown leaves across the grass of the haugh and into the stream, calling-cards of autumn. Some fluttered through the hole in the hand-fasting stone until that was obscured by Milada's body bent back over it, like a sacrifice on an altar, clutched by Patrick, propped forward out of his chair and lifting himself up on his arms..

Ruth assured herself she wasn't snooping. She had every right to come looking for them, needing them to get down to work on this campaign Matthew had brought in. But when she looked down the slope at those two ecstatic bodies she could hardly shout some everyday phrase at them — 'Time for work,' or 'Break's over'. To take even a few steps closer would be to break the spell.

And what revenge might Patrick take on her tonight when she was asleep and vulnerable? Ruth felt herself walking along the fringe of another dream, this one taking her along the edge of a Shakespearean production in a sheltered glade, or an open air concert.

Bethany Critchley's voice broke the spell. 'Garden of Eden stuff? So long as we're not expected to go down and pick up their clothes. Or fig leaves.'

'Jealous?' Ruth twitted her.

'After what he did to Josie? Not likely.'

Patrick was pressing Milada further and further backwards over the stone as if to break her back.

'I think we'd better leave them to it,' said Ruth, and thought how banal that sounded. 'I imagine they'll be back soon.'

'Certainly can't keep up that pace much longer.' Bethany took a deep breath and said: 'Look, Mrs. Saltram, I'm sorry, but I'm afraid I shall have to give in my notice. I don't like what's going on. Being shoved aside to make way for that . . . oh, whatever she calls herself.'

'Bethany, I'm so sorry. But you can't

leave us, just like that. I know things have been a bit weird, but — '

'I'm sorry, but I *can't* stay.' She turned towards the house.

Ruth hurried to catch her up, gasping a plea for her to wait and talk it through.

Matthew intercepted her. Emptying his briefcase of documents marked *Confidential* and his latest toy, a new iPad, he burst out: 'I'm beginning to think I'm being followed. Three times this last few days there's been a car on my tail. A big white Mazda.' He slammed the empty briefcase. 'Maybe they're keeping tabs on *all* of us.'

Ruth felt uneasy. Predators circling Burntrigg, checking on the occupants' movements, seeking a gap in the defences?

Before they could pursue the question, Patrick and Milada came back to join them, glowing, somehow in a different world from anybody else. Yet alert and ready enough to discuss whatever Ruth and Matthew put in front of them, with Hugo to one side monitoring his protégé's progress.

'Right. Let's see what our customer has

in mind.' Matthew indulged in his usual fussy handing out of the documents he had so painstakingly amassed.

Ruth tried to concentrate, distracted by her awareness of Hugo, pretending his usual detachment but today more intent than she had known him.

Intent on Milada.

The girl made an appealing picture, her skin with its sweetly peachy glow of a Botticelli, filling this dull room with light. Yet she also managed to be seriously attentive, concentrating on the matters before them.

While Hugo was daydreaming about her, visualizing her moving to and fro one floor above him — envious of the younger man who could make her move any way he chose?

The proposed campaign was a challenging departure for the Copsholm team. A group that had already gone public with criticism of the Government's fiscal policies was financing a secret programme of disruption. It was essential to swing a forthcoming by-election and get rid of a high-profile policy adviser who would be forced into resignation by revelations of bribery in local councils and between branch secretaries.

'Blatant slogans won't do,' said Matthew. 'We have to feed their propaganda into the minds of half a dozen influential local councillors and a millionaire sponsor who can tilt the scales.'

Hugo said: 'Might be worth pointing out that there's always a danger of any regional decisions or mutual deals being overridden at any stage by some Government minister.'

'Which means,' said Patrick, 'that we don't waste time on the small fry but go straight to some man near the top. Fix him right at the beginning.' He stared into infinity. 'I wonder, for instance, whether the Special Adviser to the new Minister for Regional Liaison has a yen for some lady in his own Department? They all usually have a lech for somebody or other.'

Milada smiled an awkward, reproving smile at her lover.

'Christ,' said Matthew. 'Flying a bit high, aren't we? You'll be after the Prime Minister next.'

Patrick nodded. 'Could be, when necessary.'

'Let's stick to the basic situation we've been commissioned to tackle.'

'Which is to disrupt one perversion of constitutional procedure,' said Patrick blandly, 'by introducing another.'

'Forget the ethics. We simply have a commission to fulfil.'

Patrick said: 'I'm more than ever coming to believe there are better ways of spending one's time. Much more fruitful ways.'

'I wish to leave this degrading job.' Ruth held her breath.

'And just what else d'you think you'd be capable of?' Hugo demanded.

'I fancy a freelance career.'

'You can't just wander off and expect to pick up commissions on every street corner. Without someone to counsel you and assess your potential in relation to the specifics — '

'It is time, I think, we use our powers for good.' Milada spoke up with quiet intensity. 'For healing. Do you not see?' She was appealing directly to Ruth. 'You could be helping us to organize all our energies to help the sick. We have the power to administer simpler and more effective anaesthetics than any chemical compound, and we are better equipped to ease the recovery afterwards. There are so many diseases we can conquer by sheer concentration. So much pain we can spare the elderly and the infirm. No need for drugs. And we can dream drug addicts off *their* lethal addictions.'

'And Big Pharma will just love that,' said Hugo waspishly. 'Not to mention the drug-running gangs.'

Matthew produced one of his most characteristic snorts. 'You'll be wanting us to publicize ourselves as psychotherapists next.'

'Better that,' said Milada, 'than indulging the ambitions of misguided politicians, and businessmen, with all their corruption and wickedness.'

Patrick's expression was no longer that of the devoted lover. 'Oh, don't overdo it, lass. You don't have to take wickedness all that solemnly. It can be so rewarding, watching the idiots squirm, listening to their caterwauling. And sharing one's own

295

appetites. The throb of pleasure, deep down in the blood.' He was daring her to argue. 'Only weaklings are scared of evil.'

There was a long, shuddering silence. Then Patrick nodded imperiously at Milada, and she positioned herself to push his chair towards the door.

Hugo watched them go; and then was tense, listening to the sound of the stairlift.

Ruth's temper snapped. 'You fancy her, don't you?'

'Good God, I wouldn't dream of it.'

'You mean you wouldn't dare. Least of all in dreams, with Patrick on the prowl.'

'Look, I'm simply sorry for the poor child. From my room I can hear things. It shouldn't be like that.'

'Making you randy, eavesdropping?'

'I'm talking about the . . . the sound of a whip. And there are those vicious red weals right down her back and over her bottom.'

'Just a minute.' Matthew was wide-eyed. 'How could you have seen that?'

Hugo flushed. 'It was just by chance. I happened to be on the stair when she came out the other day. On the way to the bathroom, I suppose . . . and I . . . well . . . '

'You indulged yourself in a few choice fantasies,' said Ruth.

'Those marks were real. Then there were the sounds. The lashings. And her crying.'

'Just a minute,' said Matthew. 'Where on earth would he get a whip from?'

'Mrs. Storey,' Ruth said, thinking. 'While she's been out shopping. Always takes a list of his requirements.'

Hugo said: 'Damn it, it would never have struck me that that woman would be capable of — '

'You've been too busy looking at just one woman and daydreaming about the eternal triangle to notice another inter-secting triangle.'

'This is no joke.' Hugo was losing his usual detachment. 'That ungrateful young lout. After all I've done for him. I suppose he considers himself too big for me now.'

'You've supposed all along that we've been using him. I did warn you he could be using *us*.'

There was a tap at the door. Carolyn

Finch-Mordaunt put her head round it. 'There's a Professor Sedlák in reception. Says he's come to visit his daughter.'

'We don't know any Professor . . . what was it?' snapped Matthew.

'Milada's father,' said Ruth.

Before Matthew could make any further fuss, Hugo said: 'Leave this to me.' He stalked out.

5

Hugo Lanner settled their guest in his best armchair before fetching the drinks tray from the cupboard. Priding himself on his ability to make an assessment of anyone at a first encounter, he was swiftly adding fragments of immediate impressions to those already gleaned from Milada Sedláková's occasional remarks during her stay here. Now at last was a chance to discuss the realities of the situation with another worker in his own esoteric field. The man must surely, in the same way, recognize Lanner as his equal.

He poured a vodka and tonic for the guest, a large malt for himself, then started formally. 'Professor Sedlák, I have the impression that we work in the same field. It's high time we exchanged ideas, I think.'

'I am thinking the same also, Dr Lanner.'

'To be quite frank, none of us had any

idea you were actually in the neighbour-
hood. But now that you've shown up
here — '

'I am here to ask why we have heard
nothing from my daughter.'

'We weren't aware she had you in the
background. Showing up out of the blue
the way she did. These youngsters — finding a job without consulting her father
first?'

He left Sedlák to judge the hint of
scepticism there, and sipped his whisky.

The Professor made a leisurely ap-
praisal of the room; nodded approval at
the Mondrian which Lanner had brought
with him to Burntrigg and hung on the
wall above his desk.

'We knew, of course, that Milada had
sought employment here.'

'In fact you sent her here?'

'She had already made her own
contact,' said Sedlák blandly.

'Which was what led you to us? And
something special about our organization
— or *somebody*?'

Sedlák probed: 'I think that perhaps I
know more about your operations than

you do about mine, Doctor.'

'Commercial confidentiality of our kind is not too difficult to penetrate if you're determined. But just why should you be so determined, Professor? What are you involved with — Secret Service, MI-something-or-other? Intelligence?'

'That word might surely apply equally to the two of us.'

'Working along similar lines, yes. With similarly talented staff. In your case, a member of your own talented family.'

'Family, yes. Not acquired by kidnapping.'

'Some unpleasant concepts about our methods seem to have got around.'

'Coping with misleading concepts is one speciality of my colleagues and myself. And trying to cure them.'

'By breaking a prisoner in body and spirit in order to wring confessions out of him, whether they're true or not?'

'Dr. Lanner, you are making some dangerous accusations. Has a certain member of your staff been — trespassing? Mentally trespassing on dangerous ground?' When Hugo hesitated, Sedlák went on: 'Come now, we both know that we are discussing a most unusual phenomenon. Whether these remarkable talents should be applied to matters of commerce or to the defence of one's country — '

'Or to the destruction of other countries?'

The Professor made a show of appreciatively downing the remains of his drink, and made no protest when Hugo provided a refill. With the same deliberation he said: 'The efficient running of national political and military systems nowadays depends less and less on coping with the enmity of another warlike country. The real threat comes from breaches of cyber security within one's own territory. Viruses, calculated denial-of-service infiltration. In a few seconds it can put all our electricity grids and communications satellites and military controls out of action without firing a shot or needing to get within thousands of miles of a conventionally targeted installation.'

'And the anti-viral defences?'

Sedlák gave a sly nod. 'We talk about the same thing, do we not? Something which few people out there know about.

Something which both our organizations wish, each in his own way, to manipulate.'

Hugo confronted his guest directly. 'The fulfilment of dreams? More potent than the commonplace realities that both our organizations wish, as you say, to manipulate.'

'We admit, I think, that we are both fascinated by the potential. So much more so than with all the other current obsessions. Mobile phones, iPods, all the absurdity of the worldwide web, with people of limited intelligence exchanging their banalities. Not realizing that the really significant communication is between minds attuned to deeper realities. How many people understand that their mobile phone sends out signals that can be used to track their every movement? The police use what they pick up without even bothering to ask a judge for a warrant. Where you are going, who you are seeing . . . Yet in spite of all that technology, they still cannot predict terrorist attacks.'

'Whereas the unimpeded mind — '

'The minds of the Gifted Ones can reach into the very depths of the human soul. Can predict, can control. Dreams were here long before men began to send out these twitching electronic banalities. Interpreters of dreams have always been revered.'

'Or persecuted.'

'Too true, Doctor. But the dreamers of dreams — the consciously controlled dreamers — are now learning, are they not, to control their enemies more efficiently than those dabbling with what one might call the modern witchcraft of scientific devices. We seek a control more subtle and destabilizing, and far less easy to counteract.'

'Unless — '

'Unless there are operatives with the same gift, trained to neutralize those intrusions.'

'And perhaps trained,' Hugo objected, 'by elements within a country's military system to attack dissidents not just mentally but physically. Using dreams to infiltrate and cripple all opposition.'

'But think of the potential for good. If someone had been able to foresee *from inside* exactly what Stalin, Hitler and the like would be capable of, and could have stopped them ever coming into those ideas or into maturity in the first place by adjusting their minds, or contriving an accident in childhood — '

'Or suppose,' said Hugo, 'that the Gifted One is himself a potential Hitler? Or mass murderer?'

Sedlák's head turned, momentarily distracted by a creaking noise outside the door.

Milada came quietly in. Not, this time, pushing Patrick in his chair. Patrick was following, propelling himself jerkily and aggressively: guarding her, Hugo wondered, or jealously ready to guard his own interests?

Her father said: 'My dear, your friends have been asking after you.'

'Friends?' It was little more than a whisper. 'I am not so sure any more about friends.'

'My poor child.' His reproachful moist eyes turned towards Hugo. 'What have you done to my little girl?'

'She's been happy enough here, haven't you, Milada?'

Professor Sedlák sounded all at once commanding and wheedling at the same time: a father with a difficult child, not altogether sure of his authority. 'I think it best you come away and we talk. You come back with me now.'

'Leave? But I am not ready. Not yet. And I was supposed to take Patrick with me. Is that not so?' She sounded both confused and bitter.

Hugo jolted as if he had been kicked. 'The hell you were.'

'But I have not wished to take him anywhere.' She had all the wistfulness of a vulnerable child who had dreamed of treats and then been disappointed. 'I wished only for us to be always together.'

'And now?' Hugo looked from one to the other of them, waiting for a sign of their togetherness, for Patrick's reassurance to the girl.

Patrick said: 'I won't be going anywhere with her.'

'So that's that. Milada can stay here and — '

'Let her go,' said Patrick. 'She's no further use to me.'

306

6

How had the ground underfoot become so treacherous? One moment he had been walking along the street, trying to remember where he had left his car, the next his feet were slipping and stumbling, and the pavement was tilting to and fro. Everything was out of proportion, illogical, irrational. He was not himself. He was not where he ought to be.

I must get a grip on myself. Too many things happening all at once. But I've always been able to cope before. Why is all this happening now — and how do I find my way out of it, when nothing's in the right order?

He simply couldn't remember where he had parked the car. That was ridiculous, since he had always been able to find a place in the public car park below the marketplace, and only a moment ago he had been looking at one of the market stalls. He would have to catch a tram back to Burntrigg. Only they hadn't had trams in Heddleburn for years — not since long before he ever came here to live and work.

Suddenly there it was, in a gutter. He hadn't thought of looking down at that angle. Because it was only about half the right size. Even as he watched, it threatened to compress itself into the size of a Dinky toy.

My car . . . He began to cry. But Dr Hugo Lanner, distinguished parapsychologist, never cried. Grotesque.

He stopped on a corner to buy a morning paper from a newsstand. But the man selling them didn't seem to see him or hear his request.

And since when had there been a newsstand on that corner in Heddleburn?

It occurred to him that he didn't even know which street this was. He felt dizzy, and wondered if round the next corner he might find something familiar to steer him back into normality.

There was a woman on the corner. He said: 'I'm sorry to bother you, but I need your help. Am I right in thinking that — '

She walked away.

Milada Sedláková was waiting at the next corner. Only when he came up to her did he realize that he could see through her clothes and see the dried blood patterns on her body, as if she had been subjected to long hours under a cat-o'-nine-tails.

While somebody, somewhere, was deriding him with a hoarse laugh that grew louder and louder and encircled his whole head as he stumbled across the road and turned a corner, then another corner, and found himself in a snack bar he might have visited before. Only this time, just as he reached for a slice of ham and a tomato, the man behind the counter told him that it had been ordered by somebody else and there was nothing further available.

He lurched home. Only how had Burntrigg been transplanted into the heart of the town? He wanted to get to bed, to lie down and sort things out in his mind. But he couldn't find the wheel stair. Only a dull flight of stairs going straight upwards into darkness. He must be in the wrong house after all.

Yet Ruth was there. 'Look, where's everybody gone?' he asked. Only she was staring right through him, not registering his existence. 'Where's my room?' he begged. 'Look, I just want to lie down. Where's my bed?'

A mocking voice was saying, 'Goodbye, and pleasant dreams.'

Somehow he was at last back in his car and driving home — only hadn't he already reached home? — and as he headed into a familiar roundabout he was confronted by a huge hole in the road. He tried steering round it, only to find himself on a precipice to his right. The car was pulling over, fighting against him, and the bonnet was beginning to head for a hideous drop. Patrick's voice came from the back seat, jeering, urging him on. Hugo tried to reason with him. 'After all we've achieved together. Everything I've done for you. You've got to help me now.'

Then he was sliding out of bed, standing shakily upright for a moment before heading for the bathroom, woken by the need for a pee.

It was morning. Too early to start work. Too early for breakfast. Nobody else would be awake.

Except for somebody, somewhere, who was sniggering close to his ear, but silently. Only how could anyone snigger silently?

Where was everybody? What happened to that ungrateful brat Patrick, and that girl, the girl with the sweet pink flesh lacerated by red stripes . . . ?

Now he knew. He had been rejected, tossed aside. Patrick was finished with him.

When at last there was somebody to speak to, he said: 'What are we going to do? About *him*?'

'More to the point,' said Ruth, 'what is *he* going to do about *us*?'

Hugo struggled to keep things in focus, to make sure he was now really awake. 'Where the hell is he? Let's have him down here and put things on a proper footing. We've been too slack, letting him get away with — '

'He's gone.' Matthew was seething with more than his usual impatience. 'The

311

nerve of the bastard.'

'Gone?'

'Walked out on us. Or been lured out.'

'He can't get far.'

'He's taken Mrs. Storey with him,' said Ruth.

Training her, thought Hugo helplessly. Stealing their housekeeper. No compunction, no gratitude. 'He's been training her. Visiting her at night, I'll bet. Grooming her in dreams. Creating a willing servant for himself.'

'They can't get far,' said Matthew desperately.

* * *

Muir said: 'You mean he's given us the slip? Cleared off?'

Milada's always quiet voice was choked with tears. 'He has gone, yes. Would not listen to me. Says he will work his own way from now on.'

'Bloody hell. But where's he gone to?'

'I have lost him,' she said simply.

'You did say you always knew where he was. So where's he making for right now?'

Dr Sedlák said: 'Please, I think she is under too much strain. She has been misled and — '

'Looks as if we've all been damn well misled. But,' Muir hammered away at it, 'you did say you would always know. So?'

'I shall try to find him. But I think he will . . . shut me out.'

Muir drew in a long, shuddering hiss of breath.

'That's one hell of a loose cannon out there.'

Part Five

CANTRIPS

1

This is not how it ought to have been. Not the way I originally planned it. It ought to have been Milada and I leaving together, setting up together, pooling our resources and calling the tune for those nonentities who need the guidance of us Gifted Ones. For that is what we are: gifted beyond the normal human imagination.

They thought they owned me, Dr. Hugo Lanner and that Saltram woman and their sidekicks. Their own pet freak, provided with a comfortable cage and a food bowl, brought out every now and then to go through his tricks for their entertainment — and profit. Expecting me to go out visiting on their behalf, breaking into people's dreams the way another employee would make an appointment and show up with glib sales talk. And once Milada had come under the same roof, she could be pampered and exploited in the same way.

The time had come to leave.

I'd believed that the two of us belonged neither in their shoddy world of business executives nor in her father's world of espionage and grubby politicians. That's all too crude and so pathetically easy to manipulate. There are greater challenges to be faced.

Yet with all that potential, the sad creature proved inadequate. Early on she haunted my dreams and I walked into hers full of hope, but she was unworthy of me. It was all a sentimental dream. I of all people should have known it was a tawdry illusion. She had no concept of the need to be ruthless, of the inseparability of pain and pleasure. Her misguided inner stubbornness wouldn't let her come with me on the terms that ought to have enriched us. She talked all the time of our powers of healing, of curing people of so many diseases. In the end there's no cure for anybody. I've dipped into so many dreams, such a morass of longings and frustrations, and deep down they are all contemptible.

So for the time being, unfortunately, I

had to use what shoddier material came to hand.

'You *will* call me Elaine, won't you?' Poor creature. Poor Mrs. Storey, so easy to convince, with dreams so easy to shape. Once I had realized that Milada had forfeited any possible role in my future, I subjected Mrs. Storey to intensive grooming. Starting with visits to her in dreams, I steeled myself to follow it through at snatched moments in daylight.

I am Patrick Robson. I owe loyalty to no one but myself. I am the one who says when and how my talents shall be used. But there has to be a transitional phase while I shake off the dross I accumulated from the Copsholm exploiters, clear my mind and let it explore freely. I will need patience. Irksome, but it must be more than just marking time. I must exercise my powers so that even the most apparently trivial moment yields something of ultimate value.

I had been given my own bank account and debit card for withdrawals from a machine. For a time Dr. Lanner had supervised it, but when I grew impatient with this, he humoured me by allowing me to use Mrs. Storey as my go-between as she was making routine purchases on my behalf in the town. I checked that he was not still carrying on a surreptitious check on my withdrawals. He was so anxious to make me feel that he was my respected mentor that he was glad to pamper me in that respect.

Whenever Mrs. Storey was out shopping on my behalf, I arranged for her to withdraw in five separate transactions as much cash as could be removed without arousing suspicion, and made contact with the helpers who were waiting for me out there. They had been driving round the Shire, making a number of reconnaissance, testing the viability of possible pick-up points; and had finally chosen the crossroads two miles south-east of Burntrigg.

We timed it for an afternoon when the Copsholm directors were deep in one of their earnest conferences. I knew there would be a full hour before they condescended to call me in to decree what part I was supposed to play, believing that they were all the time the ones pulling the strings.

Mrs. Storey was wheeling me out for a spell in the fresh air. We were delayed in our planned escape route by that tiresome Carolyn creature watching from the terrace as she finished a glass of fruit juice. When she had gone back in, we were on our way to the car park. There the CCTV might be recording, but like all such feeble safety precautions it would tell what was happening only after it had happened. I eased myself into the passenger seat of Mrs. Storey's second-hand Fiat, she folded my chair and heaved it into the boot, and we headed for the crossroads.

The car awaiting me was a large blue Honda with drop-down seats in the back, which could comfortably take me seated in my chair. Two of the men I had summoned from far across Europe greeted me with a respectful smile and a charming sort of little bow. I appreciated this. It ought to set the tone for our relationship. Comradeship . . . but respect.

We left Mrs. Storey at the crossroads. It was a pathetic sight, the poor creature watching as I prepared to leave without her. She had believed she was going to be with me forever. She began to cry and struggled to utter some feeble protest, but then simply leaned back against the side of the Fiat and stared with a puzzled frown at the scenery. It was a transformation I had expected. Indeed, I had planned it — injected it into her dream the night before while she thought I was murmuring words of quite deplorable passion into her rather ugly ears.

My timing has been perfect. I have wiped all hope and a wide swathe of memory from her mind. We left her there to get her breath back, and drove south.

And here we are.

* * *

Our headquarters is to be this pleasant little shop in a small town five miles inland from the North Norfolk coast. A quarter of the houses here are holiday homes, but there is none of the pretentiousness of the coastal resorts. Residents are comfortably indifferent to their neighbours.

They are used to strangers coming and going, some passing through on their way to the sea, some staying awhile without ever settling.

In my case, a few people I pass in my wheelchair will give me an awkwardly sympathetic nod or, more often, look the other way in embarrassment.

Our building is deceptively large behind that unobtrusive shop front. There are bedrooms for the five of us, two with en suite bathrooms, a good kitchen, and a large lounge with a grand piano under the window.

The shop itself is, of course, a music shop.

Colin Kennedy has been running it, largely as a mail-order business, for five years. That was how I had made this most useful contact, searching the dreamwaves for my favourite music, and finding myself in harmony with a man whom I recognized at once as one of the Gifted Ones. He was honoured by my confidences, and only too willing to help establish a cell of the like-minded — or, as one might put it, the like-talented.

So now, pooling our resources, here are the five of us: Dinu from Romania, Alain from the Camargue, Luigi from Sicily, Colin from the Outer Hebrides; and myself. We are not like those operators who make a show of turning their backs on the city and working from the countryside with their computers and laptops and search engine. We need no machinery. We have enough concentrated power to communicate whatever we devise to whoever we wish to receive it — and listen in to the answers without their knowing we are there.

The night of my arrival I indulged myself in deep, contented slumber. In the small hours I drowsily bestirred myself and went looking for Hugo Lanner, to give him a last taste of my abilities and wave him the sort of mocking farewell he deserved.

From now on I shall be the one in charge of my destiny — and the destiny of many others. The shop will provide a small regular income until I can find some way of extracting money which the Copsholm exploiters surely owe me, and what remains in that special account opened by the benevolent Dr. Lanner. They will doubtless try to block it. Sooner or later I must concentrate on making their nights a torment until they release it.

Over these past few years I have learnt to sleep lightly. That way I can slip in and out of a dream, skip from one to another if I'm bored; and escape if I'm in any danger of giving too much of presence away. I had also practised deep meditation while at Burntrigg, but there were always too many petty interruptions. I did no more than flex my muscles, as it were, for the benefit of other people's pockets. The challenges were often entertaining enough in themselves, but of little lasting significance. I have a destiny; and nothing must stand in the way of its fulfilment.

At our first full meeting I explain to my chosen acolytes the basis of a programme, triggered by that recent local government plot which Mrs. Saltram and that grotesque Matthew Armour had been considering.

'It can only be considered as a first tentative step,' I emphasize. 'The overthrow of the present corrupt system can't be achieved overnight. But if we concentrate our minds on one carefully chosen target after another, pursue each one to its logical conclusion, we eventually reach the crucial factor. Using one small constituency as a springboard and exposing some skilfully planted tales of corruption, we create an opening through which we can infiltrate.'

'In each political upheaval in my country,' says Dinu, 'there has always been a clash between different racial interests. It has been necessary to eliminate dissidents and establish a framework within which each must conform. Too much time can be wasted on discussion.'

'But too many deadly mistakes can be made,' says Alain warily, glancing at me for my approval. 'Too many revolutions have caused too much unnecessary bloodshed and in the end achieved the opposite of what was intended.'

Stealing a leaf from the Copsholm book, I draw attention to the record of a local MP with an apparently safe position as Under Secretary of State in the Ministry of Defence. Six months ago he fought off an accusation of bribery in secret dealings with an American arms manufacturer, fortunately overshadowed by three much more serious and well authenticated charges against two of his senior colleagues who had been claiming excessive grants for houses which they claimed to be their main residences while letting them out to Far Eastern millionaires at considerable profit. Such trivia; such grubby little misdeeds. But leaving so many vulnerable, when one knows how to exploit the opening.

Dinu is all for immediate action. 'We eliminate him. We concentrate, we have what we may call a séance, is it not? And we extract his secrets, and destroy him, and replace him with own choice. From then on — '

'Take it easy.' I won't have anyone rushing headlong into aggressive action. As a group we must learn to combine our resources at full power when necessary. At the same time, it is understood that when I wish to be alone I am to be left alone for uninterrupted contemplation.

Colin has been deputed to buy me a

powered wheelchair. On a fine afternoon I can venture out on my own, as a rule keeping to the back streets. There's only the faintest likelihood of anybody passing through who might recognize me and report back; but there's no point in taking unnecessary risks.

Once we have achieved our ends and are in a position powerful enough to strike down all enemies, there will be no need for such secrecy. But I am prepared to be patient.

Unlike Dinu, who is capable of disobeying orders. And unfortunately I have allowed it to happen: I have allowed myself to be distracted.

One afternoon on my way back from a brief trip in my wheelchair I let myself be tempted to go in through the shop instead of using the rear entrance to our quarters.

A young woman was talking to Colin about music for her piano. She admitted with a warm little laugh to spending most of her earnings from a daytime office job on different recordings of Bach suites and chunks of the 48. I couldn't resist the lure of joining in the conversation with my opinion that the whole lot sounds better on a harpsichord. She argued — and argued very brightly, very charmingly. I enjoyed her flushed enthusiasm, and the brightness of her eyes, and the tremor of her breasts as she grew more and more impassioned.

A few days later, from the corridor behind the shop I heard her ordering a version of Alban Berg's Lyric Suite. Colin had it waiting for her the following afternoon, while I was looking idly through other CDs on the rack. As she paid for her purchase, she glanced at me uneasily.

I had in fact visited her the night before, insinuating into her sensually receptive mind the lovely hidden meaning in Berg's work — the pattern of HF and AB dancing seductively in and out, rejoicing in the passionate secret affaire between the composer and Hanna Fuchs-Tobettin.

The whole thing lasts a week.

In the small hours of our next night together, she wakes up crying, trying to sit up and reach for the bedside light.

'What are you doing to me?'

I put my arm round her. 'I hoped you'd enjoy that.'

'No, I don't ... I ... you creepy ... '

The light comes on, casting shadows further afield than the non-existent walls of the dream room. She pulls away from me. 'You must have put something weird in my drink.'

'Not into your drink,' I say. 'Directly into your mind. Which was very receptive.'

She wriggles towards the edge of the bed. 'I'm going. I'm not staying here.'

As I've said, it lasts a week. Each day she has come into the shop and looked around, willing me to come in yet afraid that I might do so. When I am there, she darts quick, disbelieving glances at me, with fear and then with yearning. Each night she denies what is happening; by the middle of the next morning is mutely begging for more.

It has been a distraction, which I ought not to have allowed myself. Like a bout of physical exercises, it has kept me in trim; but in what might be called my absence — in that I have not been paying attention — Dinu has taken action on his own.

★   ★   ★

Our targeted MP has a son with a share in a trawler based on one of the fishing villages facing the North Sea. For some weeks the boat has not been allowed to go to sea because of some restrictions on herring quotas. While laid up, it has been due for long neglected repairs. But one night recently the young man has been restless in his dreams. Longing to be out at sea again. He has urged the rest of the crew to join him, and they haven't taken much persuading.

They go out into a swell that threatens a storm within hours. The boat becomes waterlogged, and sinks two miles offshore.

At the same time a suspicion arose in a local marine safety officer's mind about the operations of a rival fleet of trawlers five miles further along the coast. Documents were released to show that the MP, stricken as he was when interviewed in newspapers and on TV on the loss of his

331

son, nevertheless had a large share in that other group. There was talk — the sort of talk that creeps from one fishing community to another like a slow incoming tide — of the father's callousness and, the way some folk saw it, family problems which had long since soured their relationship.

'Won't take long to unseat that one,' Dinu crows. 'Then we can move our own pawn into play. Or our bishop, perhaps?'

He has expected me to be pleased. I've had to make it clear that individual forays of that kind can be no part of our programme.

They may be irritated by the slowness of developments. But we can aim at the top only by working our way very cautiously around the foothills. The Prime Minister is ripe for toppling; but that can't be done at one fell swoop. Not right now, anyway. I am the one who summoned these others. We go into combined action when I say so, not before. If any of those I have chosen turn out to be inadequate or rebellious, I shall be the one to halt them and, if necessary, dismiss them.

Lying down one afternoon to meditate, I drift into an unexpected place. Not for the first time, I have wandered into somebody else's dream, left carelessly open to a trespasser. And here, slightly out of focus, is Milada.

She is wandering, unsure of her surroundings. That uncertainty makes it difficult for me to keep her steady enough for us to talk. The overwhelming impression I get is one of unhappiness, yet below that there is another level, one of expectancy, a joy that she hopes will overcome her doubts and reproaches.

Reproaches? Against *me?*

I want to reach out, get my arms round her, offer her the chance of working with me again, freed of her childish doubts and her even more childish flinching from our shared ecstasies of pain.

She is narrowing her eyes, clutching her stomach, thinking of something else in which somehow I am involved.

Then somebody is trying to blot her out — or is it *me* who's the target?

Dominic Lynch. Dragging her away to the side of the picture. Blurring her. Like one sticky hand clinging to her and dragging her off, while the other hand is pushing me back.

I fight. But then Milada seems to be giving in to him, and the two of them together are enough to block me.

And out of the haze comes one clear, solid certainty. This is the moment when I realize that Milada is pregnant.

So treacherous. Cunning, concealing it from me. Closing her mind so that I could not read what she knew.

I find myself trying to shout, but the words thicken in my throat.

Someone else is taking on shape, urging her not to listen. I am to be cancelled out. Oh, no, they don't comprehend what they're facing.

She can be persuaded — partly against her will, partly because of her own weakness, her stupidity in not committing herself to me — pressured into not listening to me. But my son in her womb . . . *you* can't be persuaded like that, can you, Patrick my boy? Because Patrick is to be your name, and you will have to come along with me, growing inside her body until it is time to come out into the world which comes to seem reality for most newborn children. But you will be one of us, Patrick. As the child of Milada and myself you cannot avoid your wonderful destiny as one of the Gifted Ones. I will be by your side in our shared dreams, and you will be a key part of the future I am planning. Until then, lie there in comfort while I implant in your already receptive mind all that you must know and understand.

It is to you that I am dictating all these memoirs. It will all be stored in your mind ready for when you burst into the world, and grow up, and take over where I leave off.

And you will understand why the perverting of your mother by those in charge of Dominic Lynch must be stopped. I have long had a score to settle with Dominic Lynch, and before anything else I think I should get that distasteful little matter out of the way.

I try to call the two of them to stay still and, for their own sakes, listen. But they are dissolving into the background of that drab room. Only one figure remains. Not that dismal little father of hers, not anyone military.

The tall, unfathomable shape occupies that remote corner of my vision where I have glimpsed it so often before but never been able to command a clear response. For the first time the head seems to have turned slightly, and I think I might get a glimpse of the profile; but it's as uncommunicative as ever.

Yet somebody is speaking. Not so much a voice as a ghostly reverberation.

'It is almost time for you to choose'.

2

The other day I came across an advertisement for a sweetened plaster used to kill cockroaches by solidifying and hardening them from within. It's an idea that appeals to me. I am wondering on whom I could practise something like this.

Meanwhile, I find it harder and harder to work with my four colleagues. I fear I'm not cut out for collaboration. Some of the time they are too impatient, wanting overnight successes; at others, they dawdle, dabbling in what I can only call psychic conjuring tricks — the sort of thing I long ago grew out of.

Such as Alain indulging himself with that lecturer at the local town hall.

All week a banner across its façade has been advertising a display of Aztec artefacts, on tour after an exhibition in London. I've passed it a number of times, but I couldn't get my wheelchair up the town hall steps. I found myself inside the building only when I stumbled two nights ago into one of Alain's dreams.

The elderly lecturer is just starting his amble from one display cabinet to the next. His reedy voice speaks with spluttering enthusiasm of the children ordered to cry as they were led to meet their death so that their tears would become rain to water the earth. Flecks of spittle blow from his lips as he describes the Aztec custom of flaying people alive to provide robes for their priests. Those priests, suitably attired, could then set about tearing out the hearts of young devotees, offering the blood splashing up the walls and running down the steps of the temple as a willing sacrifice to the gods. When a couple of women turn away disgusted from some of the grinning masks, the lecturer hastens to say: 'We must not judge people of that era by our own standards. They were perhaps not as deliberately cruel as we might think. Sacrificial victims went to their death gladly. Quite probably in a drugged trance.'

That night Alain thinks it will be entertaining for the man to experience what he has so far lived through only in those crackly-voiced perorations. It takes some time to find his dream world, and for me to catch up with Alain. Unsure of his own powers, he has the wretch tearing in his sleep at his chest and stomach with yellow fingernails. The effort is too much, the old man is fighting back. I have to add my strength to Alain's to get those nails digging deeper, turning red with blood. He starts howling some appeal to a god — not an Aztec god drinking his sacrificial blood, but the God of his local church childhood, backed up by a painting on his Sunday Schoolroom wall.

We have no need to check in the local paper to be assured that he has been found dead in bed after what could only be assumed as a violent bodily spasm or internal haemorrhage

I have made it clear to Alain that such self-indulgent individual forays are not to be repeated. The others pretend to remain innocent of the whole problem. But I'm beginning to worry whether I can trust them.

I am telling you all this, my son, so that you will know what kind of world awaits you. As you lie there warm in your mother you will gradually begin to assimilate what I am dictating to you now. You will have to carry on where I leave off. So listen, young Patrick — for that is the name I insist on for you, whatever anyone else may try to decide.

I come into your pre-natal dreams with love. Though I must be honest with you — with you, above everybody — that it is often more entertaining to play games with silly people. Practise on them, build up strength from each game you contrive to win. Then later you can face the greater challenges awaiting you. Asleep you will find yourself, like me, able to float above the world, or some interesting chosen corner of it, not so much looking down to study it as drifting contentedly until something plucks at your attention and you can swoop . . . or gently insinuate yourself. You will learn and know.

Night after night I have wandered through a blur of dream fantasies jostling one another like argumentative stallholders in a street market. There can be sudden flashes of brilliance as a wild, desperate love or hatred breaks through the swirling fog of colours and noise — feeling — feeling the tension of nerve-racked limbs, the throbbing of anguish in a head, the torments of indecision and of wrong decisions, tossing and turning in bed until wakefulness brings relief and at the same time a draining sense of loss.

Some minds are more receptive than others, almost eager to be provided with a goal of horror that they can reach, and wake up from their nightmare raring to go. Others take longer to break them down. You will learn just how easy it is for those of us with the gift to interpret or wilfully misinterpret the wishes of ordinary folk. To give them what they think they're asking for and then watch their realization of what they have really brought down on themselves.

In dreams people indulge themselves in thoughts they wouldn't dare to contemplate when wide-awake. If you can catch them in their intensity of dream, and push them . . . Oh, imagine what it is like to have them at our mercy. Come on, share what I have in mind for you. And wake up screaming in unison with the true joy of terror.

Such as that which I have just imposed on Dominic Lynch.

You will ask why I forbid Alain and the rest of them to indulge themselves in personal forays, yet have no scruples about tackling one myself. Firstly, there can be only one man in command of enterprises such as ours. And secondly, Dominic and *his* associates are a menace to what we aim to achieve. I have floated around the outskirts of their world and grown to know them too well — just as I have known Hugo Lanner, and now suspect that those two factions are capable of joining forces and presenting a real danger to me.

Especially if they can persuade Milada to work with Dominic against me.

It's time to strike.

I have tried a number of times to eavesdrop on those secretive anti-terrorists holed up in Prestwick, but there have been barriers. The minds of creatures like Brigadier Muir and his immediate staff are difficult to penetrate for the reason that there is really nobody there. They have all been brainwashed by the very tenets of their own employment. But Dominic and your mother: a different resonance altogether, and at the same time a different problem; they are far too acutely aware of the possibility of infiltration, of being overheard and interpreted.

Which is why they have put up automatic barriers against me. Whenever I try to breach them, their alarm bells ring, they are alerted to the danger, and the two of them in concert have the power to shut me out.

But at last I am finding my way in. They are in the company of somebody else, discussing a possible collaboration, and so diluting their defences. My old mentor, Dr. Hugo Lanner, no less. And with him, Professor Pavel Sedlák. They have so much in common, those two: so many high-flown theories to toss to and fro, that there was bound to come a time when they would get together.

They have all been too busy to prevent me easing myself in. I shut myself away for an afternoon sleep at a time when

Dominic is having his own sleep after some 'special rendition' has just gone through, and he has been urged by Sedlák to clear his mind, preparing it for some enterprise which they will discuss when he wakes. They are a much more skilled team than the one I have assembled, in spite of the talents I had hoped to nurture.

Dominic's overtired mind drifts, against his longing for a blanked-out sleep, onto a question of documents. In the secret archives of Brigadier Muir's administration are records of all the interrogations carried out over the last three years. Almost as fanatically scrupulous as the Nazi concentration camp commandants, the Secret Service cannot resist the lure of keeping meticulous accounts of every name, every torture session, every mutilation and every death under their aegis. And now there have been leakages. A newspaper has demanded an investigation. A commission of enquiry asks for the documents. Hastily it is declared that such revelations would breach the Official Secrets Act and endanger the anti-terrorist campaign.

The whole thing must be hushed up. Not just a matter of destroying the evidence, but of Muir's team invading the minds of at least two influential cabinet secretaries and twisting them out of shape, so that they let themselves become scapegoats, while releasing a few insignificant Top Secret papers and throwing the hunters off the trail.

I add my own little distraction, planting even more warped suggestions into Dominic's contemplations, like a suicide bomber's device timed to go off at the crucial moment.

And to fill in the waiting time, I pay a visit to Hugo Lanner.

He recognizes me as I come into his sleeping vagueness and steer him into his study. 'Get out, you! You're not really here. I do know that.'

I lean on his desk. 'If I'm not really here, how do I get out?'

'Look, Patrick, I know you have this ability to project certain aspects of yourself, but — '

'What's all this rubbish?' I breathe over the papers on his desk, and they begin fluttering about. 'Is this the best you can do?'

'Leave them alone. You wouldn't understand this sort of work.'

'It's fit only for the flames.'

I persuade him to crumple up some of the sheets and toss them into his waste paper basket. He works himself up into an argument, but then begins muttering, 'Oh, all right, all right' and 'I can always start again' and reaches for his cigar lighter and sets fire to a bound typescript. The dream expands, becomes a ring of fire, and then dies to no more than a few glowing embers. I release him, and he wakes up and of course will try to dismiss it; but the bewilderment goes with him.

And I have ensured that the fire will go with him.

But now, out of nowhere, my mother comes visiting.

'Patrick, what are you doing? My child, what have you *done*?'

★   ★   ★

What, indeed, have I achieved?

It would appear that there has been a serious conflagration in one of the huddle

346

of freight warehouses at Prestwick airport. Statements about the cause and extent of the damage are bland and uninformative. 'Commercial confidentiality' — where have I come across that mantra before? In the meanwhile, two local employees have been seriously injured, but the extent of those injuries is uncertain, and Ayr Hospital is not yet releasing any details.

The newspapers would surely enjoy the pictures I could conjure up for them. I had, after all, foretold the whole scenario, though it turns out to have even more dramatic consequences than I'd expected.

Inside the building declaring itself the property of Steerforth Import/Export Freight, Brigadier Muir is bellowing orders, enjoying the reverberation within the large assembly area. Lined up against one wall are two vans specially equipped for the transport of prisoners and their guards to and from the far end of the airport runway, and a small, compact fire truck. Against the opposite wall is a long rack of equipment whose uses are known only to specialists.

Muir glares around, and then barks the signal to begin.

An industrial-size shredder is manned by a Lieutenant Slee and watched with a sort of distant contempt by Dominic Lynch. In some perverse reasoning typical of the spooks, it must have been decided that although the documents are to be destroyed before any court in the land can demand their appearance, he is deputed to memorize key factors as they flip past him into the shredder. I am not sure how deeply his abilities can dip into this, or what sense it makes anyway, but there the poor dismal wretch stands. Slee springs automatically to attention as a pallet stacked high with documents is wheeled towards them. Dominic bends towards the first batch.

And loses his balance, as I have made sure he would.

The machine shrieks as the first sheets run into its maw. And then it emits an even shriller, more grating sound; and Dominic's howl is added to the cacophony. Groping to regain his balance, he has clutched the edge of the machine, and slid his fingers into the teeth. It jars back a few feet under the impact with a tooth-aching screech of metal along the concrete floor, belches a last guttural hiccup, and stalls.

Ah, the music of bone grinding against bone, splintering and being crushed together! The sound of blood bubbling in the throat, the particularly exquisite sound of a human gasp of disbelief that so much pain is possible — a gasp on its way to a shriek.

Smoke begins pouring out of the machine. Muir and Slee wrench clumsily at the control, and succeed in ejecting what remains of Dominic's crushed fingers, dripping blood as he totters backwards.

Still the smoke curls upwards, and gouts of thin flame lash the papers left on the pallet.

It takes two or three minutes to get the fire truck into position. Two or three minutes too long. The smoke swirls and thickens, and acquires a life of its own. A black spiral claws out towards Lanner and he inhales it desperately, almost as a man might gulp down a glass of water. It swells inside him, permeates him, begins to solidify in his lungs like a black cancer.

Black, like the greedy thrust of smoke streaming up through the extractor to create a quite unforeseen aftermath.

A plane of holidaymakers homeward bound is coming in low, heading for the runway. Smoke and grit rasp into the engines and spray the windscreen. The pilot may just stay in control and set his plane down on safe ground. A matter of seconds. But then it comes — the impact, and a vast gout of more smoke and flame; and a hundred and fifty men, women and children are dead.

Unfortunate. Not foreseen.

* * *

My mother is saying: 'It's time to stop, Patrick. You're misusing your talent, and there'll have to be a reckoning.'

Unexpectedly I want to reach out and touch her, be touched by her — held close, as she had held me when I was little and she murmured such affectionate things to me. But today we're not within touching distance: we are met on that astral plane where only those of us with this gift can communicate.

'I'd hoped when you escaped into the hands of those people in the Shire that you would be content. You'd been saved from the viciousness of that circle of military plotters — '

'No thanks to you. You ran away and left me.'

I had a moment of detachment, conjuring up a vision of those two dabblers, Lanner and Sedlák, pontificating about a deprived childhood, abandoned by parents, which would explain so much to their tidy little minds. And after all that, me being so ungrateful to Dr. Lanner!

When words come, they seem to be dragged out of her reluctantly. 'It was considered best to let you go. You were deemed . . . not to belong.'

'Deemed? What sort of word is that? And who's been doing the deeming?'

For a moment I have the sensation of being drawn up to the surface, about to wake up against my will — or against my mother's will? But she is going on: 'We thought it would be enough to take you away from that school once we'd learned its true purpose. We did what we thought was best.'

'What *you* thought was best? That man' — I find it impossible to call him father — 'walked out and left us, and you went after him rather than stay with me. Then never allowed me to get in touch with you.'

'He needed me.'

'More than I did?'

'Yes,' she says simply.

So why is she bothering to contact me now? Remorse? It's too absurd a concept, and my voice makes that clear — only it is not my voice, but a direct communication between the two of us. And the response comes flowing into my mind in a welter of reproaches from some authority claiming that I once belonged to them but have betrayed their trust.

'You are a descendant of the Gifted Ones.' It is an incantation. 'I tried to warn you, all that time ago. Our Watchers continue through the centuries without a formal church, no pyramid of officials. The Wardens of the Wyrd are nowhere and everywhere, as they have been since the beginning of time. They issue no dictates. But at times it is their duty to warn those with the gift if they are misusing that gift.' The level tone becomes suddenly accusing. 'Cheapening and tarnishing it.'

'So what are the penalties?' I ask sceptically.

'Don't mock, Patrick, I beg you.' It is my mother's own voice again. 'It is enough that the Watchers disapprove.'

'Is it, now?'

'It may be decreed that you have sullied the power you hold and that there should be . . . an adjustment.'

'Meaning I've been a naughty boy and — '

'Even at this late stage you may be offered the power of recompense. Which may not be taken up by your . . . your victims. Much will depend on what they think of you, and what they are prepared to forgive. Or whether they walk again.'

'Victims?'

'How else can you describe them? Your self-indulgent persecution of that slip of a girl, your trapping that wretched businessman in his own childhood nightmare,

and just now venting your spite on others
. . . with death to so many innocents.
Time and again showing off — '

'Showing off? Who to? To myself?'

'Yes, that's the saddest part of it.'

'Look,' I say very loudly into the
nothingness that surrounds us, 'I didn't
ask to be born with this talent — or
affliction. Don't blame me if you don't
like the results.'

'We who have been privileged to carry
such precious talents down the ages have
a responsibility . . . '

Have I been reunited with my mother
simply in order to be scolded as a
naughty child?

As if to challenge her, there is forming
a backdrop of other beliefs from the past.
Other forces are tugging at me, offering
justification for all my own dream
ventures. Old fertility cults, whose ritual
killings were arranged so that the blood
would run down into the fallow earth.
The shedding of blood by Druids who
predicted the future by stabbing a man
in the chest and seeing how he writhed in
his death throes. And Christians, as

cannibal as any primitive tribe, drinking the blood of their God.

At least some of those old truths seeped through into the new religions. Above all, the truth and joy of suffering. The joy of pain and inflicting pain. After a war there are reports of the traumas suffered by survivors, mentally crippled, haunted by the horrors of death and injury, the filth, the fear. But that's not true. What leaves them gutted is the *lack* of fear of imminent death. While the conflict was on, there was the joy of killing, the bravado, the comradeship in destruction, the rush of blood to the head and the rush of blood from severed heads and limbs. Hate is inspiring. Terror is a healthy flow of adrenalin.

From the jumble of beliefs and superstitions the figure that begins shaping itself beyond the insubstantial blur of my mother is that of another woman. Too crude and obvious, I manage to think in the confusion of it all. So many religions taking the same pattern, from far, far back. Always the goddess thrusting in to take precedence. And founder of them all, the Wyrd, the quintessence of creation long before human beings began inventing their gods.

I make a more determined effort to wake up.

But there is a worse nightmare.

★ ★ ★

Already, so soon after Dominic Lynch got what he deserved, there is talk in the night waves of Milada marrying him. She would not have been coerced into doing so before, but now she is prepared to do it out of pity?

Oh, no, I can't face that. The obscenity of that creature giving his name to my son . . . No.

Despite the agony of his racked body, the wretch is really beginning to dream of that possibility. He is so weak that his dreams are now wide open to me. I can't resist tantalizing him with a foretaste of their wedding night.

Poor weakling, he no longer has even the faintest chance of holding me at bay. If he dreams of fulfilling himself in Milada, I reach him and throw him off balance. While he anticipates pawing her submissive yet unresponsive body, I get a grip on him. Hopelessly he tries to fight off the visions: to start with, a starkly clear sequence of Milada's face beginning to dissolve, as it will in old age, shredding away from the cheeks into wrinkles and sagging, putrefying flesh, transforming that demure smile of her gentle lips into a rictus of bone and teeth, while her sleek, sweet-smelling body rots around its emerging skeleton. Look at her, Dominic. Take a good long look . . .

It might be fun to provoke Milada, too, with quite other visions: to remind her of the way we made love, and how she writhed in ecstasy as I planted our son deep within her. But she blanks me out. She is so much more adept than Dominic is, so much more talented. Yet so misguided.

But for her stubbornness we could have gone out into the world together, fought off any rivals, gone marauding together in the night hours and reshaped a thousand dreams. At first she had enjoyed so much — the pain that made her cry out and beg me to stop, yet left her hunched up, the marks on her glowing with their own special radiance, an ecstasy we ought to have gone on sharing. Instead there was all that talk of using our combined talents for the easing of pain, not inflicting it.

Patrick, my son, I am sorry your mother has proved unworthy. But she must bear you, she will bring you up, and I shall be always watching. And you must be always listening. I shall be around *somewhere*. Trust me.

★ ★ ★

Fading, my mother pleads: 'My son, for your own sake, take heed. And remember that it's in the power of the Wyrd to summon the dead to walk again.'

In the corner of this dreamworld, the watching, listening figure seems to grow more substantial and turn inch by inch towards me. The woman's face is now only half obscured. I wonder what, when she turns to look at me full face, her expression will be. This is *my* dream, yet I have no control over this one part of it. No way of silencing that voice.

'*You have chosen.*'

3

They have betrayed me. I suppose I should have seen it coming; but they have grown cunning, learning how to hide themselves from me until they were ready to strike. If they have truly come from families of the Gifted Ones, those must have been tainted branches. I am furious with myself for having been so gullible as to regard them as potentially kindred spirits.

So I am here at the crossroads. Here, where they picked me up during the escape I had planned from Burntrigg, they have brought me back and dumped me, then driven away without waiting to make any formal handover.

Handed over to whom? I can pluck enough shreds out of their minds to guess that they've done a deal to toss me back into the place I came from.

But there is nobody here to accept the transfer.

Perhaps the Sedlák clique and their new Copsholm allies want no part of it. After what happened in that warehouse, both Lanner and Dominic Lynch are too scared now to let me near them? They are going to leave me here to drown in this appalling downpour?

I can't believe that. They need me.

It must be that the downpour has deterred them. They're prepared to keep me waiting until the skies clear. 'Do him good.' It could be as crude as that. I've always known that I've been dealing with simpletons, people of mediocre concepts.

The torrential rain is lashing against me from the west. Crouched in my wheel-chair, I twist my head away from the gale and try to focus on the few yards to a sheltering tree on the verge of the road. Water spurts up from under the wheels. I skid, swerve violently to the right, come to a halt facing down what I know to be the road to Burntrigg.

I am not one to be kept waiting. I despise them, I want no part of their machinations, but if this is a challenge set up for me I am ready to confront them.

My powered chair will, its instruction leaflet claims, do fourteen miles on one battery charge. I will go and confront them.

Trying to see my way onwards through the rain, I am obsessed by the invisibility of what would have been clear and spacious in sunshine. What a suggestion to dangle in front of the heavy-handed minions of Brigadier Muir, if he's there with the Copsholm faction. Not that he's really in charge of anything much. Orders filter down to him from puffed-up men with ridiculous titles and code letters instead of names, signifying something hush-hush, forever demanding a break-through in a scatterbrained theory. So here's one for them . . .

Invisibility. How's that for a wonderful weapon of war? Not difficult to impregnate someone in dreams with the defect of passing somebody next day without even seeing them. In battle, massive application of the technique could make one's forces invisible to the enemy, which could lead to . . . well, just consider the wide-ranging potential. After I've dropped the notion into the minds of Muir's minions, they'll surely be in a hurry to ingratiate themselves with the top brass by reporting back to that hidden place in the US where military planners are still staring at goats and dabbling with subliminal sounds.

I have so much to do. So much to achieve. I'm only just beginning. I could do without the interruptions of these persistent phantoms, shapes steadily badgering me, shapes right now forming themselves out of the downpour, windblown, hunching sideways, spasmodically reaching up and then swooping towards me in a vicious arc. Blurred shapes torment me, taking on distorted, derisive faces.

Abruptly I find myself faced with a fork in the road. To the left is surely the direct way to Burntrigg. But a deep flood is bubbling across it. To the right must be the winding lane that dwindles to a mere path along the bank of the stream.

Going in through the back door? I know that route so well, uphill from the haugh and its stone. Something is drawing me on. I am meant to face this, meant to confront whatever awaits me at the stone.

Milada? So that I may reason with her, dismiss her fantasies? Seek absolution? Lay claim to my son . . .

My son. Patrick, are you listening? Assimilating all this, storing it up against a future in which I may be taking no part?

The low-lying ground beside the stream is increasingly soggy. The wheels of the chair squelch through mud, spin a protest, come to a stop. A thin film of water lies on the haugh, and the handfasting stone has become a diminutive rocky islet with a waterfall streaming down its flank.

With its Lorelei draped across it, slowly becoming lustrous in an evening glow through the rain.

Milada, waiting for me. Summoning me?

I try to urge the chair onward, but it is stuck. I push myself up, out of the seat, stumbling one step forward. My feet plop in the mud, but I force myself towards her.

And her face becomes that of Josie McCann, grinning. A wide grin, from the suppurating face of a cadaver, the teeth snarling in hideous ecstasy. The gaping bite marks I had left on her breast and shoulder spew snakes whose stabbing fangs are preparing to launch venom into me.

This is the warped vision of a dream. But this is no dream, it's reality: yet I'm not sure that I can any longer distinguish between them, having for so long believed dream to *be* the true reality.

I lurch to one side, try to get my balance. And the ground gives way and engulfs me.

I'm sinking. Mud closes over and all around me. Slime dribbles into my mouth. I try to keep my lips clamped shut, but there is a steady sucking and plopping sound all round me, and the mud is pushing its way into my ears and up my nostrils. I must keep calm. The weight on me is growing more and more painful, trying to thrust me even deeper into the waterlogged earth.

They'll have to come and dig me out. Can't just leave me here. I'm far too important. I'm in the direct Bloodline of the Gifted Ones. My mother made that clear. All I have to do is be patient. They'll have to come and get me out.

It may take hours to reach me. A few days, even. But they will come.

Keep listening, Patrick. From now on I must concentrate all my efforts. I must seek out the dreamers who can be made to help. Thrust my way past the mediocrities who wish me ill, find those who can be brought together to dig, get me out of here.

But there's one weight as worrying as the heaviness of waterlogged earth: the realization that nobody knows I'm here. How long will it take any of them to guess, to come searching?

They must hear me and come. Muir, Lanner, Sedlák. They need me. I am too valuable to be abandoned, left to die.

Patrick, are you listening? Can you convey a message, speak to your mother from her womb, needing no words but letting her know . . .

There is silence. Patrick, why are you not hearing me?

Another blow to trample me down even deeper into the mud.

Milada is dead.

She has taken her own life. She has dreamed herself into death, taking our son with her. It has been decreed that our Bloodline should come to an end.

There is nobody now to listen to me.

I am being left to die.

* * *

And so it has come. Dreaming and wakefulness are all one. Time is an irrelevance.

I am dead.

And I am learning how pathetically wrong you are, all of you out there, doctors and scientists pontificating about the moment when the brain ceases to function and consciousness is cut off. Not having any idea, any of you, how much longer it really takes to die. I'd never really envisaged — does anybody? — what it would be like for the mind to go on functioning while the body gradually rots away round it. Never guessed how long the mind can go on thinking and suffering long after the flesh has begun decomposing.

366

The hours go by, the days, the nights — what is the difference between any of them now? How long is eternity? I'm beginning to stink as my flesh deliquesces. A gradual, inwardly seeping stench. Something so sickening you have to vomit, yet find you can't. How, if I'm dead, can I smell this so keenly?

I only dream I can smell it. I must think myself out of it; cease believing I have any sense of smell.

Who could ever have believed the mind could take so long to fester?

It's getting worse. And all the time I'm still fully conscious.

And being haunted.

Josie again. But Josie, too, is supposed to have died long ago. Taking a long time a-dying, like me. And like some of those others. A crushed caricature I hardly recognize as a thing once called Edgar Seymour, tearing shreds of himself free from the jagged metal of a crushed Saab. And another man, an older man — oh, that old fool in the museum. He was probably in no real pain, drugged by his own self-satisfaction. A girl playing the piano — something I only half remember, yet here she is, reproaching me. Hugo in the background, groping his way out of a trance towards me, only to find his way barred by a fury of fire and smoke.

Each of them slithering towards me through the mud. I had left a trace in each. Assemble all those fragments, breathe a new half-life into them, and they become too clamorous. Dominic Lynch trying to crawl towards me, but lurching aside, floundering, 'surplus to requirements'. So he has died of his wounds?

Summoning the dead to walk again. That was what my mother had foretold.

I am being assailed from all sides. Continuously there's the gloating laughter of the worldlings who have enjoyed contaminating somebody above and beyond their understanding. Deeper down, encircling me, a deep, overwhelming sadness, the awareness of desecration.

While I lie here slowly rotting away, the reality outside, above me, is rushing unstoppably past.

Patrick . . .

I am calling into a void.

At last they are all gone, the phantoms sent to haunt me with warped memories. Now there's only a dark doorway and that one familiar yet unfathomable figure standing there, now turning slowly to look at me, full face at last. Nothing ferocious, no dripping fangs from a bloodthirsty horror film. Just a beautiful but unrelenting face. I try to persuade myself I am dreaming this all up. She is a figment of my dying imagination, that's all.

Still that face, flawless, beautiful beyond belief, stares implacably at me.

Beg for mercy?

Admit your rebelliousness. Repent.

What, like some petty little communicant going to confession? Far too late. And still too much to expect of me. She must know that.

What is the point of dictating all this, when there is now nobody to record it, remember it? No one to talk to.

Would cremation not be a kinder, quicker way to go than being laid in earth? But how can you be sure that you

369

will not feel your dead flesh crackling and spitting in the heat?

Damn you all, I'm not ready to let go. I must haul myself out of this decomposing body and in immortal dreams reach out to mix in a higher society with those who will respect me. Wandering the midnight revels, the clubs that don't advertise, the places where punters gamble with their souls.

What I might have been able to achieve if I had dared to live a daytime life in that company! The things I might have enjoyed . . .

The noise in the cavern of my skull is overpowering. Such a confusion of clashing, undisciplined minds. Like a thousand different rubbishy popular tunes being played simultaneously at full volume. I must take charge again. Damn you all. If I'm to be imprisoned here, before I go I shall create dreams which will make the whole world afraid to go to sleep.

What the hell is that laughter, rippling through me again? Hell . . . a resonating word, a fine time to let that word slip out.

Nothing solid around me any more. A

vast foetid breath rages up out of a seething void, channelled through that doorway, sucking me towards it. I am dissolving, as if the mud around me has started to simmer with a current churning me along.

No, I refuse to believe any of this.

And why the hell is somebody playing music from *Don Giovanni*, far too loud, overpowering? Don't any of you realize that I hear music in my head that goes beyond anything that has ever been written down or could be played on conventional instruments — beyond anything that *could* ever be written down. Music dancing and screaming in eternity beyond the far borders of black infinity.

But the time has come for silence. I surrender. Just let me sleep now. Really sleep. A true, eternal, dreamless sleep this time. Let me just cease to exist.

That watching woman has lifted her arm to beckon me towards that doorway of darkness.

A woman? No, surely not. A *thing*. An intolerably bright image of vengeance, unyielding, radiant in terror.

No, this I'll not believe.

371

She can't exist.

No, I'm not going to look over that edge. I refuse to believe. How many more times? I *refuse*.

Nothing can be so foul.

I am being sucked towards the edge. I'm going to be ingested by what's been waiting for me. But I shout, scream, yell soundlessly that I deny all this, I will not be bludgeoned into believing, into retracting, into succumbing . . .

Stop *staring* at me. Stop that relentless beckoning.

No, I refuse. I deny you. *I deny* . . .

THE END